W9-BMR-327

Slowdown at Sears Point

DONATED
BY HALF
PRICE BOOKS

Slowdown at Sears Point

Ken Stuckey

Baker Books

A Division of Baker Book House Co
Grand Rapids, Michigan 49516

© 1999 by Ken Stuckey

Published by Baker Books
a division of Baker Book House Company
P.O. Box 6287, Grand Rapids, MI 49516-6287

Printed in the United States of America

All rights reserved. No part of this publication may be reproduced, stored in a retrieval system, or transmitted in any form or by any means—for example, electronic, photocopy, recording—without the prior written permission of the publisher. The only exception is brief quotations in printed reviews.

Library of Congress Cataloging-in-Publication Data

Stuckey, Ken
    Slowdown at Sears Point / Ken Stuckey.
        p.   cm.
    Summary: Two teenage boys share their interest in NASCAR racing and their faith in God at the Save Mart/Kragen 350 at Sears Point International Raceway.
    ISBN 0-8010-4149-X
    [1. Stock car racing Fiction. 2. Christian life Fiction.]
    I. Title.
    PZ7.S93757S1 1999   99–40587
    [Fic]—dc21

Scripture is taken from the HOLY BIBLE, NEW INTERNATIONAL VERSION®. NIV®. Copyright © 1973, 1978, 1984 by International Bible Society. Used by permission of Zondervan Publishing House. All rights reserved.

For current information about all releases from Baker Book House, visit our web site:
                    http://www.bakerbooks.com

Acknowledgments

THANKS, GING. You are the greatest gift that God could give me. Thanks, Sam, Stephany, and Katie, for your awesome encouragement. Thanks, Eilersens, for your encouragement. A special thanks to the folks at the Napa Valley EFC for participating with us in this adventure.

Introduction

A NASCAR Winston Cup stock car race is a big event. In some respects it is a lot like the old-time circus rolling into town with its garishly painted wagons full of strange and exotic animals. Except in Winston Cup racing the wagons are 80,000-pound haulers that carry their own brand of strange and exotic animals. Brightly painted animals that take special care and nurturing to fully exploit their capabilities for speed and power.

The business of racing has become increasingly popular and is now a multibillion-dollar industry. Big-name sponsors and famous drivers bring big-time notoriety, and the media celebrates and records all aspects of the event. The fans come out by the thousands, showing loyalty to their favorites with T-shirts and caps, coffee cups and belt buckles. They fill the grandstands and infields to overflowing with an excitement that is loud and opinionated.

By Saturday the field is set for Sunday's race. Advantage and adversity have no doubt played a part as the cast and characters seek their positions on stage, for every race is a drama.

The final act is played on Sunday afternoon, and when all is said and done it boils down to one thing: which team and driver have blended the proper amounts of sweat and perseverance, good fortune and experience, to seize the victory. For there can only be one winner.

Do you not know that in a race all the runners run, but only one gets the prize? Run in such a way as to get the prize.

1 Corinthians 9:24

"I want to win. That's what it is all about."

Jimmy Spencer,
Winston Stock Cup driver, car #23

ORLY MANN CASUALLY reached up and wiped a drop of sweat off the end of his nose with the back of his gloved hand. It was hot, but not unbearably so. At least not yet. He was waiting patiently for the pit marshal to give him the go-ahead signal to fire up the car and begin the first practice session of the weekend for the Save Mart/Kragen 350 at Sears Point International Raceway. Orly liked this track.

The race season kicked off at Daytona Beach in February with the prestigious Daytona 500 and concluded in November at Atlanta Motor Speedway. In between, the movable circus that was The Winston Cup Series visited twenty different racetracks with thirty-one different races.

In thirteen years of Winston Cup stock car racing, Orly had won the championship twice. In between he had managed to win thirty-three races, which was truly remarkable considering how close the competition had become. But last year he won nothing except the "hard-luck" award and spent the last third of the season rehabbing from a fractured leg and facial burns collected at the Mountain Dew Southern 500 at Darlington. He had not qualified well and had gotten involved in a twelve-car, middle-of-the-pack, pileup through no fault of his own. Sometimes stuff happened, and when it did it hurt.

The pit marshal rubbed his fat stomach, then suddenly reached up and pressed the radio headset against his ears. He nodded his head, tugged the bill of his red baseball cap that said "Official" across the front, and circled his finger in the universal signal for "start 'em up." Orly flipped the toggle switches that activated the fuel pump and ignition system and then pressed the starter button. The starter ground a couple of times, and then the finely crafted racing engine blasted into life, shaking the car with an even rumble. There was nothing genteel about the sound of a race car. Particularly the sound of a stock car. The unrestricted exhaust headers dumped right underneath what would have been the left door of a regular car and the sound resonated through the body and filled the air with acrid exhaust.

Orly gave the dash an intense look and carefully studied each of the gauges. The oil pressure was where it was supposed to be and the oil temperature gauge was coming up right on the money. The flat circular faces of the other gauges were telling a similar story. The water temp was coming up—in this heat it wouldn't be long before things were at optimum operating temperature. A racing motor needed a certain amount of heat to function in the way it was intended.

Orly glanced around the inside of the car and examined the pristine, almost antiseptic, interior. Everything was painted a light gray and Orly sat in the midst of a series of bars and tubes called a roll cage. The light color was on purpose so any leaks or flaws would be immediately discernable. This might look like a stock car on the outside, sort of similar to the one Mom and Pop drove to the office and supermarket, but in truth it was a thoroughbred, highly crafted single-purpose flat-out full-time race car designed to fit within the rules of the NASCAR book . . . and it was Orly's office.

NASCAR enforced the rules with a brutality that was designed to enhance safety and keep the competition even. Sometimes it seemed a little heavy-handed, but it worked. Stock car racing was the most exciting, evenly matched motor sport in the world and it attracted millions of fans. Orly's life was busy with a schedule that was often grueling and sometimes overwhelming. Public appearances for sponsors and media bytes with an ever increasing fan base made ordinary existence tough if not impossible. It seemed like somebody always wanted a piece of him in one fashion or another. That was one reason Orly liked doing his job, which was making this race car go faster than anybody else's. Once he climbed in the window and strapped himself in the custom-fitted seat, the outside world faded into insignificance. Racing was his job, and now it was time to go to work.

He eased the car into first gear and gently slipped the clutch as he passed out of pit lane and idled up the hill through turn one. Sears Point sat nestled in the Napa/Sonoma Valley surrounded by vineyards and beautiful rolling hills, which were blowing golden brown in the gentle summer breeze. This was Friday, and this was the first practice in preparation for Sunday's race. The 1.95-mile track was surrounded by grandstands which on Sunday would be packed to capacity with over a hundred thousand people. Stock car drivers raced mostly on oval tracks, but twice a year they visited two road-race circuits. One at Watkins Glen in New York State and here at Sears Point.

Sears Point was the toughest. It had a new format this year that demanded a precise driving style. It was nearly two miles of changing elevation that was hard on brakes and tires and tested a car's handling. Pure horsepower helped but a driver had to know how to turn right as well as left, something oval tracks weren't good at teaching. Many a transmission would be turned into a pile of case-hardened junk as drivers sought to mix skill with speed. It was a track that was a genuine test of a driver's ability, and Orly loved it.

As Orly cruised up the hill warming things up, the voice of Bear, his crew chief, filled his head through his custom-fitted earpieces, which not only brought him the radio transmissions from his crew but kept the rumbling and sometimes shrieking exhaust noise bearable. Sometimes it seemed Bear was sitting next to him yelling in his ear.

"Don't forget, Orly, we got that new tire compound on. You might want to make sure you got 'em warmed up good before you get on it. Someone said there was a little oil left on turn seven from this morning's amateur practice."

Bear was a worrier—sometimes he was worse than a mom sending her boy off to school for the first time. Of course Bear worried. He was a crew chief, and that's what crew chiefs did mostly. They worried. They worried about the car and the driver and the ten thousand things it took to make a stock car competitive and a driver able to drive it at optimum speed. Then after they worried a while they fixed things and made them better. Well, in theory anyway.

Orly keyed the mike button bracketed to the steering wheel twice, which meant he understood. Even though he sat alone in the race car, Orly was never really alone. He was in constant communication with his crew. He was also monitored by the NASCAR officials and more than likely at least 70 percent of his fellow competitors.

Bear, who neither looked like nor acted like his name-sake, knew this too. Just like he knew that there was probably no oil on turn seven and that there definitely was no new tire compound. A new tire compound would get their competition's attention because it would be an unfair advantage, and he liked to tease anyone listening in. Stock car racing not only involved racing against the racetrack with the best possible equipment, it also involved racing against a lot of other drivers and crew chiefs who were wise and crafty in the pursuit of the ever-so-difficult first place victory that paid the most money.

Bear operated on a very simple basic philosophy— somebody had to win and it might as well be them. Bear was a rather shy, rotund, blond-haired blue-eyed, five-foot-eight-inch normal looking guy. He possessed a keen mind and a fierce loyalty to Orly. He and Orly had been together for eight years, and both had made a lot of money racing cars. Bear's given name was Henry Erickson, and he was one of those unique individuals who had the ability to make others see his vision. He knew how to motivate and had a unique style that was all his own. Orly knew for certain that Bear could get more out of a crew than anybody else in the whole world. Bear seldom if ever raised his voice but by example, and bright-eyed interest and a sense of humor, put forth boundless energy. On any given day he could outwork any three guys on the team and they knew it and respected him for it. His nickname "Bear" came as a direct result of the crew's love for him.

Pit stops played a big role in any NASCAR event. Tires and fuel were renewable resources, and the car could only go so many laps without stopping. When it stopped, the speed of the crew was critical. The quicker the car was serviced with new rubber and a fresh tank of fuel, the quicker it could get back out on the track. Many a race was won or lost by the abilities of those that went over the wall to refresh the car. As Orly would come thundering down the pit lane in the course of a race the quiet voice of Bear would echo in the crew's headphones with the admonition, "We got to bear down, boys. We got to bear down and do this one right." This meant that everyone had to do their particular job with the utmost speed and efficiency.

It wasn't long before Henry became "Bear," and now everybody, including Orly, called him that. If the truth be known, Henry liked it and even signed his autographs, "Bear Down," or simply, "Bear."

Bear had a long association with Orly and had respected his abilities as a driver even before they started the team. He also had great love for Orly as a friend. Theirs was a unique relationship that had been tested many times through the stress and rigors of competition.

Orly didn't like talking on the radio much and made no effort to fill the air with small talk. He and Bear had perfected a code over the years in which they could exchange information about what the car was doing without giving anything to the competition. It was a simple "yes" and "no" that was signaled by the number of times Orly clicked his "send" button on the steering wheel of the race car.

Jimmy was another matter. Jimmy was Orly's spotter, which meant that he usually sat high above the racetrack in the tallest building with all the other spotters and fed Orly information about who was where and if there was a yellow flag out, and whatnot. At Sears Point, Jimmy, along with the other spotters, sat high up on the hill that overlooked the whole track. He had a pair of binoculars and could see almost everywhere except the pit lane, where Bear could keep Orly apprised of what was happening. Jimmy had a critical job—he often had Orly's life in the palm of his hand. In the event of a smoke-filled crash, it was Jimmy who told him to go high or low, inside or out. At 200 mph in a place like Daytona or Talladega, with wrecked race cars spinning all over the place and the air full of acrid tire smoke, Jimmy's information could mean the difference between a destroyed race car and a hurt driver or a trip to the winner's circle. Here at Sears Point it was a little different. Since Sears Point was a road course, Jimmy's primary job was to give Orly a bird's-eye view of what was happening. *Jimmy is certainly high enough to do that,* Orly thought .

Jimmy liked to talk, and sometimes he drove Orly nuts with his off-the-wall comments made in his slow Texas drawl. He was also totally unflappable. Orly had never heard him raise his voice, even in the midst of the most trying circumstances. Once Orly had hit the wall at Bristol and torn the right side of the car to tatters. He had hit so hard that he ricocheted across the track toward the pit wall. He was sliding along at a terrific speed, trailing a large stream of sparks, totally out of control with no brakes, no steering left, and the pit wall coming to meet him like a freight train at a bad crossing, when Jimmy's voice said in his ear, "You better duck, Orly."

Some spotters considered themselves coaches and treated their drivers as if they were giving birth to kittens, filling the air full of constant exhortations like, "You can do it" or, "Come on, baby." Orly always said he didn't need a coach, he just needed a spotter. And Jimmy was one of the best.

Orly idled the car up the hill into turn two, a sharp right-hander, and gradually picked up speed as he worked his way through turns three and four. He came out of four, feeling the little rise in the track that would get him almost airborne at race speed and headed down what the new track owner and promoter so affectionately called "the chute." It was a downhill sweeping 890-foot straightaway that dropped into turn seven.

Turns five and six were part of the old course and not used by the Winston Cup cars. Orly missed them because it was a section of the course that separated the good from the excellent. The good cars would barely stay on the track as the drivers sawed the steering wheels trying to maintain control. The excellent could use this opportunity to pass and pick up spots. If nothing else it had been a great place to gain time.

This new section was going to be interesting come race day. Dropping down the hill the car had a tendency to get loose, and it was hard to set up for the tight turn seven. Getting through the corner wasn't the problem. It was exiting the corner while maintaining the delicate balance between speed and control. Too much speed and the car would carry to the outside and into the dirt. Once in the dirt the driver had to fight for control and do his best to stay out of the gravel pit—which was designed to slow the car—and the ultimate indignity of slamming into the tire barrier and destroying the car.

Orly gave a casual wave to the corner workers as he made the turn and headed downhill through the esses. Located on every corner there was a flag station with highly trained volunteers, led by a person called a corner marshal. The job of each crew was to let the drivers know what was going on in their particular part of the track. When a corner worker waved a yellow flag it meant there was trouble of some sort there. If a driver crashed or spun the car, these crews were his first line of defense in keeping other race cars off him. Their job was to warn and protect. In a place like Sears Point, which had several "blind" corners, these folks were not only a necessity but a blessing. In the event that a driver crashed hard enough to be hurt, they would be the first to get to him. Every corner marshal was equipped with a knife to cut stuck seat belts and harnesses, and they wore gloves in the event they had to drag an unconscious driver from a burning car. Every corner crew had a trained firefighter with at least two bright red fire extinguishers, and they were in constant communication with Race Central Dispatch.

As Orly came through turn seven he entered his favorite part of the racetrack. This part of the track was fast, even faster now with the chute. Turns eight and nine were just little twists in the road as the drivers blasted down off the hill. To go really fast, the driver did his best to keep the car in a straight line with his foot on the throttle and let the track unwind beneath him. This meant that he must lay the car over the sloped curbs that indicated the inside and outside of the corners even though they had a tendency to lift the car into the air. After the car crested the little rise at turn nine and dropped down the track, there came the papa-gut-grabber turn ten. This was a corner in which a driver either made time or lost it. It was one of those corners where every instinct told the driver to lift his foot, but experience and blind reliance on mechanical technology overruled common sense as he pushed the car for more speed. The car carried an awesome amount of momentum off the hill, which made this corner "flat-out." Here the entrance had to be absolutely precise or the driver would run out of track before he ran out of corner and find himself plowing into the Armco steel barrier protected by a row of strapped-together tires. The old tires cushioned some of the shock but not a whole lot, and many a car and driver wore the bruises to prove it. Anybody that had ever tried to get around Sears Point at full speed had at least one and possibly many scary moments in turn ten. It was what race car drivers called a "separator"—it separated the men from the boys. And handling it wrong could get a driver separated from his senses. Turn ten also set the stage for the last corner—turn eleven. If the driver got through turn ten with the proper line then he was carrying a whole trainload of straight-line speed into turn eleven.

A Winston Cup driver sat low in the race car, and the sensation was a lot like driving straight into a very substantial solid-looking wall protected by a tire barrier. Leave the braking too late and he played "come and get me" with the wall. Brake too soon and he could get passed on both sides and feel fairly foolish as he exited the corner. Leave the braking a little late and he would dive too hard to the inside of the corner and end up swapping ends in a cloud of tire smoke and brake dust. The proper line was to leave the braking as late as possible, make an early apex on the corner, and let the car run out right next to the pit wall under acceleration heading for the start-finish line.

At least that was the way it was supposed to work. Turn eleven had a propensity to get oiled pretty good, and a good driver always had his eyes peeled for the shiny spots on the track, which meant less adhesion and could mean disaster. The old race driver saying "Beware of the grease mud for therein lurks the skid demon" was fairly applicable on a regular basis in this corner. It was a great place to pass if the driver had the brakes. Many a race at Sears Point had been decided by a last lap shoving match as the cars came off the corner, jockeying for position.

Orly fishtailed the car, putting some more heat in the tires as he exited turn eleven and keyed the mike button on the steering wheel.

"You ready, Dougie?"

Eighteen-year-old Doug Prescott stood atop the transporter parked in the long line of trucks in the garage area. The transporters were essentially movable shops called "haulers." They were as large as any semi-truck on the road and as recognizable as any race car. Each one was garishly painted in the same color scheme as the race cars they ferried. They were as clean and almost as finely crafted too, and in their cavernous trailers they housed all the spare parts, tools, and tech support that it took to carry a team and car through the weekend. They brought everything from clean uniforms for the crews to extra engines, transmissions, and rear ends for the race cars. Housed on a hydraulic ramp in the top of the trailer was a complete, track ready, spare car. The primary car was generally parked behind it and it usually wasn't touched unless there was a major disaster. In the pits, or working garage area, the trucks were parallel parked in a long line so close together one could almost jump from the top of one trailer to another. Every team had an observation platform built on top of the trailers and it was here that owners, team managers, and various support personnel observed the proceedings on the racetrack.

Doug leaned against the rail of the observation platform with the radio headset on his head and a clipboard with three digital stopwatches built into it resting in front of him. He reached down to his waist and keyed the transmit button on his radio to answer Orly's question.

"You bet, Orly. Let's get it on."

"Okay, kid. Be sure and get some differentials."

It was Doug's job to keep track of Orly's lap times on the racetrack. He would also use the other watches to get various times from specific corners, which were called differentials. Orly and Bear would later use these times to see if one particular line was working better than another as they made subtle changes to the car during the practice session. It was a big job for a kid, but then Doug had been around racing most of his life and he knew what he was doing. His dad, Bud Prescott, worked in Orly's shop and was one of his most trusted employees—second in command to Bear. Something had happened that Doug did not completely understand and it seemed that his dad had disappeared one night, leaving his mom, Doug, and his sister alone. He had left without telling Doug anything and his mom wouldn't say anything, other than, "It'll be okay, Doug. You know your dad will come back when the time is right." Doug didn't even know where he had gone. Doug was still trying to sort it out. Orly had suggested to his mom that Doug travel with the team over the summer anyway. He would be gone most weekends but home for a few days in between. Doug was a sharp kid, and Orly and Bear trusted him. Trust was a big issue in Doug's mind and it counted for a lot. A guy had to be able to count on something. Sometimes the unanswered questions about his dad drove Doug crazy. He had been gone not quite a month, but it seemed like forever. Traveling with the team was a real blessing and gave him the opportunity to fill his head with technical stuff and diverted the pain a little, although sometimes his chest pounded with worry about his dad. He loved him so much and this separation without any explanation seemed so wrong.

Orly accelerated past the pit wall, gave a little nod to the pit crew, and got down to business. Orly was pleased. It was one of those unusual situations when the car was great right off the truck. All Orly's hard work and expertise plus Bear's technical genius back in the shop in North Carolina paid off. As he worked it through the corners, his driver's intuition told him that this baby was set up well. After five laps he pulled it into the pits to allow the tire guys to get a pyrometer reading. A pyrometer was nothing but a temperature probe that was run across the width of the tire. The various temperature readings would give an indication of how well the suspension was set up and what kind of wear patterns to expect on the tires. They finished, and one guy placed a small slip of paper into his gloved hand as Orly dropped the window net. The window net was designed to keep Orly's arms and head inside the car in the event of a crash. It was also designed to keep foreign objects outside the car in the event of somebody else's crash. Orly didn't bother to look at the paper as he idled into the pits to Bear and the crew. He knew what it would say. He brought the car to a stop behind the hauler and motioned for Bear to come close. He didn't want to talk on the radio and let the whole world know what he was about to say. Bear put his head in the window and Orly yelled in his ear to be heard above the motor's roar.

"It feels good, Bear, great as a matter of fact. I'm going to take it back out and push it hard for four or five laps then bring it back and we'll check everything."

Bear answered him with a quick nod.

"Stay sharp, Doug."

Doug clicked the mike button twice in response as he looked down on top of the orange and yellow car. The stylized number 37 filled almost the whole roof area, and if he turned his head just right he could see Orly Mann written across the top of the driver's side window in a copy of Orly's own handwriting.

"Jimmy, watch me close through the esses, especially in eight." The mike button clicked twice again in Orly's ear.

This time when Orly went down the pit lane it was with purpose. He flipped his visor down and stood on the gas as the pit marshals gave him the go ahead. The tires warmed up quick, and the car began to work the way it was designed. One of the things that made a race car driver great was the ability to focus and concentrate solely and completely on the job at hand. Orly blocked the outside world and gathered all his mental and physical faculties to make this car go as fast as it possibly could. Doug watched the clock, and at the end of the first lap gave Orly his time over the radio. Orly didn't take time to acknowledge; he just buried his foot in the floorboard and slightly adjusted his line through turn one. Orly wasn't alone. There were several other cars on the track running at various speeds as crews and drivers went through the same process as Orly and Bear. A stock car had an infinite amount of adjustments possible, and it took experience, wisdom, and a whole lot of skill to come up with the right combination of gear ratios, shocks, springs, and tire pressures to make the car work best. Orly passed the other cars where he could, making mental notes in the back of his mind about corners, the quirks of other drivers, and careful observations as he pushed the car to its limits.

Orly was down to business as Doug gave him the lap time in an even voice for the second lap. It was considerably faster than the first as Orly began to shave tenths of a second here and there around the course. The third lap was even faster, and Jimmy remarked that Orly was using all the track and then some as he laid the right front wheel over the curb in turn eight. Orly decided to uncork one more fast lap and then bring the car in for a look at the plugs and a general once-over. Maybe a slight air pressure adjustment in the right front. The shocks were perfect. The track bar in the rear end seemed just right as he crested turn four, went slightly airborne, and blasted down the chute to turn seven. He feathered the brakes just perfect and nailed the apex of turn seven perfectly as Jimmy said, "Nice" in his ear. This car was really handling well. Orly was trying hard not to smile. He might even have a shot at the pole with this baby.

Orly got a good run off the esses, passed a car on the inside, and sailed into turn ten. His stomach was tight as he watched the racetrack unfold before him. The "G" force was fierce as he set the steering wheel and felt himself being pushed over in the seat. His belts were tight and he was snugged in the seat as best as humanly possible. But at this speed, even human flesh had to give a little.

Orly's foot was buried in the throttle when the right front spindle broke, instantly transforming him from the driver of a 3,400-pound "built-for-speed and tough-as-iron" stock car to a passenger aboard an out-of-control hurtling missile. When it wedged over, it locked the steering and sheared the brake line.

As soon as the suspension broke, Orly knew he was in big trouble. His instincts took over and he tried to turn the wheel. But no go. It was locked. The tire erupted in a blaze of smoke as it dragged along the asphalt. He dynamited the brakes with both feet trying to scrub off as much speed as he could, knowing that it was a useless gesture. The car slued to the outside of the corner performing a lazy half spin in almost slow motion. He had the presence of mind to hunker down in his seat, getting as low as he could. He had been here before and it wasn't pleasant. He even relaxed his grip on the steering wheel to keep from breaking a wrist on impact. There was no time for fear, only a certainty that this crash was going to be bad. Very bad. There were many places to crash at Sears Point but this was the absolute worst. Then he hit the tire barrier in an explosion of violent motion that was anything but slow. The impact against the tire barrier knocked the wind out of him and he grunted as the form-fitted seat with its wraparound design pounded his ribs. The noise was considerable, but it barely registered in Orly's consciousness. He stayed low as the car spun across the track, trailing life fluids and chunks of ripped sheet metal. He was okay until the car somersaulted. Then he lost consciousness. His last thought was, *Man, not again.*

Jimmy watched Orly through the esses, with deep appreciation at his ability to make the car go exceedingly fast. Orly disappeared into turn ten, and then he saw the sudden cloud of smoke and dust that told him Orly had crashed. He muttered to himself. Through the binoculars he saw the car come back into view, cartwheeling down the track. He waited for it to stop moving as the flag crew waved their yellow flags and the corner marshal watched traffic, waiting for the opportunity to get to Orly. The car finally stopped. It sat right side up, a mockery of what it used to be. The once pristine hand-built body was now almost unrecognizable. Clouds of steam and smoke trailed from beneath the crumpled front end. Ripped sheet metal hung in tatters, and broken parts were scattered all over the track. Jimmy pressed the mike button. "Orly, buddy, you okay? Talk to me, Orly. You alright? Come on, Orly, wake up and talk to me. Come on, Orly, put the net down." When a driver dropped the window net of his own accord it was a signal to everyone that he was okay. Well, it meant he was at least conscious and could move of his own volition.

Bear interrupted, "How bad is it, Jimmy?"

"Shoot fire, Bear, it don't look good. No. Wait. He's got the window net down. Here he comes. He's sliding out of the car now. He seems to be moving okay . . . no wait he's holding his ribs. Now he's standing up and trying to take his hat off. Bear . . ."

"Yeah, Jimmy?"

"You better get the backup car out. This one's a write-off."

Delight yourself in the Lᴏʀᴅ and he will give you the desires of your heart.

Psalm 37:4

"Nobody ever said this sport was easy. . . . We all love it and we are going to do what it takes to make these cars go. If we have to work harder then we have to work harder."
Rusty Wallace, Winston Cup driver, car #2

PAOLO HATED CHICKEN. Especially fried chicken. He couldn't stand the smell of it when it was raw in all of its pink and yellow ickiness. He couldn't stand the smell of it when it was dipped in the egg-and-cracker batter. He couldn't stand the smell of it when it was cooking in the deep-fat oil cooker, and he especially couldn't stand the smell of it when it was done and served piping hot on a bed of french fried potatoes, with coleslaw on the side. The eager customers that lined up outside the Chicken Shack seemed to like it just fine, but then they were on the outside and didn't have to smell it all day. The thing that made it really awful was that this was only Friday, his second day on the job.

Paolo was seventeen, and his uncle Rollie had just purchased the Chicken Shack at Sears Point Raceway. Rollie and a number of other vendors sold their products during the race weekends. He was experienced in the fast-food business, but this was a new venture and he needed some extra help. He had called Paolo at his house in San Francisco, talked first with his dad and mom and then to Paolo.

"Hey, Pally, howz about helping us out at Sears Point over the weekend? Help us serve up a little chicken. We'll start Thursday and work through Sunday. Give you a chance to make some extra bucks. Whatta you think? Howz about helping your Uncle Rollie?" Uncle Rollie had said in his thick accent.

Paolo's heart had leaped inside his chest. He had been praying for an opportunity to go to Sears Point this weekend. For the past three years he had watched the NASCAR stock cars come to Sears Point, had read about them in the papers, and had seen them on the local news. He'd seen the race on ESPN, but he ached to be there in person and see the cars and drivers for real. Paolo loved cars. He loved auto racing of any type and most particularly stock car racing. He was an avid student of racing and like some kids who could rattle off the statistics of their favorite baseball or football stars, Paolo could quote point standings, sponsorships, color schemes, drivers, and crew chiefs. He knew exactly where the fabrication shops were located for each team and their hometowns. He knew the track layouts and competitive lap times for virtually every track on the Winston Cup Circuit. Yet even though Sears

Point was only an hour from his home in the city, he had never been there. In fact, he had never been to a car race of any type at all. Fortunately virtually every race was televised; it was a ritual for Paolo to pop a cassette into the VCR to record every minute of the prerace, race, and postrace coverage. He also watched *SpeedWeek* on ESPN and *NASCAR Today* on TNN and any other racing program that came across the TV screen. The internet site for NASCAR was the home page on his computer, and he spent hours on the net browsing the various race car sites and assimilating as much information as he could.

The majority of NASCAR races were run in the southeast, starting early on Sunday morning on the West Coast. But church was a big part of Paolo's family life, and he didn't mind missing the live coverage. Paolo was a Christian and he liked his church. Loved it, as a matter of fact. His Sunday school class and youth group were very important to him. His love of racing was just a hobby, although a very important one. Sometimes his folks worried that he was a little obsessive about racing, but he wasn't. He just liked it. After church on Sunday he could hardly wait to get home and watch the tail end of the race. When it was over and every last interview was done, he would stop the tape, rewind it, and watch it from the beginning. *Thank you, Lord, for VCRs,* he often thought. Especially this weekend, because it seemed he wasn't going to see anything. What he'd thought was a wonderful opportunity had really turned out to be a major bust. Business had been a lot better than Uncle Rollie had anticipated, and so far all Paolo had seen of Sears Point was the inside of the Chicken Shack. If he stood on his toes and held his head just right he could look through the window and see the cyclone fence around the pits and occasionally a race car or two, but he couldn't see any of the track. Ever since the haulers came through the gate yesterday afternoon he had to resist the temptation of pressing his nose against the glass like a kid at a candy store.

Uncle Rollie's boisterous voice disturbed his thoughts, "Hey, Pally, go out back and pull some more chicken out of the outside frig. I think we're gonna need it.

"Let's get goin'. Come on, boys, a little faster. Let's get that chicken cooking! Look at those hungry customers! Here comes the money! Margarita, let's go with that coleslaw," Uncle Rollie shouted, wiping his hands on his grease-stained apron. Working with Uncle Rollie was a lot like working with a radio turned up too loud next to your ear.

Paolo dutifully headed to the back and stepped out into the sunshine, blinking in the bright light. Without the noise inside the Shack and Uncle Rollie's incessant shouting, he could hear the distant cars on the track as they continued to practice in preparation for qualifying that afternoon. There were hundreds if not thousands of people all around even on a Friday. The plaza where the Chicken Shack and the other food vendors were situated was a natural stopping point for gawkers hanging around the fence that surrounded the garage area.

Three security guards stood at the entrance, checking pit passes. No one was allowed to enter the pits without a proper credential, and credentials were not easy to come by. Race cars by nature were dangerous and putting some forty odd of them together could become hazardous. More importantly the crews and drivers needed room to work, and if everyone was allowed access to the garage area the crush of people would be overwhelming. Paolo watched as the guards turned away yet another wannabe who didn't have the right credentials.

Outside the garage area it was a festive atmosphere and people looked like they were truly enjoying the spectacle of the colorful race cars and their crews. The noise and excitement were contagious. Paolo wished deep in his heart that he could throw off his apron and join them. He would press himself up against the fence that surrounded the pits and the garage area in a hot minute, hoping to get a glimpse of one of his favorite drivers or somebody famous. Paolo took a few breaths of fresh air and paused for a minute with his hands in the band of his apron. He tried standing on his toes to see through the holes in the fence, but it didn't work. He kicked over a wire basket and stepped up on it, craning his neck for a better view. It gave him an additional two feet of height but he still couldn't see much.

So close I can smell the warm engines and hear the mechanics working, and yet I can't even see what is going on, he thought.

When Orly crashed, Doug had seen the whole thing. Well, that wasn't entirely true because his view was partially blocked by the grandstand. He had seen enough, though, to tell him that it was serious. Racing was a contact sport and crashes were fairly common and not unexpected. No driver wanted to crash but it was a fact of life when limits were pushed to the extreme, and if the limits weren't pushed . . . then it really wasn't racing. Doug had seen Orly crash before, and he knew that the crew in the shop at home would go over every detail to be sure the accident wasn't from some design flaw.

When they built a car everything was focused around safety, safety first and then speed. The roll cage was designed to certain specifications, the seat was padded and molded to conform to the driver's body, and a six-point harness held him securely within its confines. The window netting kept the driver inside the car, and everything that was in proximity to his body was padded. He wore gloves, a fireproof driving suit over the top of fireproof underwear, special shoes that insulated his feet from the hot floorboards, and a state-of-the-art helmet with a built-in radio transmitter. Every racetrack had a medical helicopter on standby just in case a driver needed to be airlifted to the nearest hospital. Every opportunity was taken to make sure the driver was safe in a high-speed wreck. When he climbed into the car he really climbed into a cocoon that was designed and manufactured out of the highest quality steel tubing that met rigid standards. Every weld was carefully and meticulously examined. Even so, the laws of physics were certain. Despite the best efforts of technology and skill, drivers got hurt, sometimes very seriously, and some had been killed. When a 3,400-pound highly crafted, hand-built machine suddenly met an immovable object like an Armco barrier, at a tremendous rate of speed, even the best safety engineering could be inadequate.

Doug stood stock-still and held his breath, waiting for Orly to get out of the car. He heard the conversation between Jimmy and Bear on his headset and was asking the same questions in his mind. He could just barely see the car around the edge of the grandstand, and he quietly breathed a sigh of relief when Orly climbed out. He was most likely bruised up pretty good but at least he was walking and talking and they weren't strapping him to a gurney for a ride in the ambulance flat on his back. He got into the emergency vehicle under his own power for the mandatory ride to the care center to get checked out by the track medical team. After an exam to make sure he was okay, they would probably let him go.

For the moment Doug's work was done, and it was best for him to just stay out of the way and keep his mouth shut while Bear and the crew figured out what to do. He decided to head back up the hill to the motor home he and Bear shared with a couple of other guys on the crew and enter the timing data he had collected into the computer. Bear and Orly would no doubt want a printout after they got things sorted out. Best to have it ready. He climbed down from the observation platform on the roof of the hauler and walked over to the little motor scooter the crew used to get around on. It was leaning against the huge tires on the monster trailer. The immense tires with their chrome rims dwarfed the little machine and made it look smaller than it already was. It wasn't much, just a little "pooter" as Bear called it, but it beat walking back and forth between the garage area and the motor home compound. Walking meant an uphill trek, and Doug much preferred mechanical movement as opposed to his own. It was always more fun to ride than walk.

Doug gave the kick starter a jump. When it didn't start on the fifth try he made a mental note to change the spark plug. Trying to get the thing started lately was becoming a nuisance. It finally took off in a cloud of smoke and rattling exhaust. Doug tucked his clipboard under his arm and headed out the pit gate, nodding at the security guards as he went by.

With an envious gaze, Paolo watched Doug ride out of the pit enclosure. He thought, *Man, that kid is cool. Probably about the same age as me. Just rode out of the pits on that little motor scooter like he owned the place and knows where he is going. Probably headed up to the motor home compound where all those ritzy motor homes are parked. Fat city. What I wouldn't give to get in the pits and spend just five minutes walking around. Would you look at that; he is wearing Orly Mann's orange and yellow team colors. He must be part of the crew. Some life I bet. Man, would I like to be him. Maybe he wants to trade jobs.* Paolo snorted out loud at his own joke. "Trade jobs. Yeah, right."

Doug passed within a few feet of Paolo, looked over at him, and smiled. As he rode by, a couple of the timing sheets slipped from the clipboard under his arm and swirled in a gentle gust of wind and exhaust smoke from the scooter. Paolo leaped over to catch them, scrabbling around on his hands and knees, yelling at Doug's retreating back, "Hey, Hey, you! You dropped some papers."

Doug stopped, put his foot down, and looked over his shoulder. Paolo in the meantime had managed to catch the papers and was looking at them intently. Doug turned around and rode back to him. He stopped the bike and shut it off, putting the kickstand down.

"Hey, these are timing sheets for Orly Mann. I saw these things on *NASCAR Today* and Ned Jarett showed how you guys use them."

Doug responded, "Yeah, they sure are."

Paolo continued to look at the sheets, "Boy, he was cutting some good times. This last lap is only a few tenths off the track record."

Doug smiled. He liked this fresh-faced big kid with a quick smile, black curly hair, and dark eyes. He seemed to know what he was talking about.

Paolo handed the papers back to Doug.

"Yeah, he was running great until something broke in the front suspension again. He crashed a little while ago over in turn ten and we think the car's a write-off. Orly bruised some ribs and got knocked around some, but he is okay. The medical people said he's okay and cleared him to drive. I haven't talked to him yet but I think he'll be alright, probably be pretty sore though. This is the fourth time we've had a piece in the front suspension break, and we can't figure out what is going on." Doug found himself opening up to this young man in an apron with a faint smell of cooking oil hanging off him and a concerned look on his face.

"You guys got a backup, don't ya? I mean everybody travels with a spare car, so you can still try to qualify this afternoon, can't ya? You guys are in the thick of the points race—you need all the help you can get," Paolo commiserated. "Can't you just roll another car out of the hauler and pick up where you left off?"

"Yeah, we have a spare, but it has a little different setup and Bear, that's Orly's crew chief, doesn't think it will be quite as fast as the primary car was." Doug took a closer look at Paolo and noted the grease stained T-shirt and apron. He glanced at the back door of the Shack and asked, "How's the chicken?"

"Oh, it's, um, ah, real good," Paolo stuttered a reply. "Hey, I'll get you some if you want, on the house, part of the perks, you know. Besides it's time for my break," Paolo said almost desperately. Anything to keep talking.

Doug thought for a minute, then nodded his head. "Sure, sounds good." He really didn't want the chicken, but in truth he was lonely and as eager as Paolo to keep talking.

"Pull up a crate and sit down and I'll bring it out in a minute." Paolo stuck out his hand. "My name is Paolo Pellegrini. What's yours?"

Doug took the proffered hand and shook it, smiling. "Doug Prescott. Nice to meet you."

Paolo grabbed a crate of chicken from the outside refrigerator and raced back into the Shack. He yelled at Uncle Rollie that he was taking a break for a few minutes and grabbed two plates of chicken and fries despite the disapproving look from Margarita. Then Paolo went out the back door, fully expecting Doug not to be there, but he was, casually going through the time sheets. Paolo handed Doug a plate and pulled up a crate opposite him.

Paolo bowed his head in a silent prayer and Doug self-consciously did the same.

"Boy, you sure got an accent. Where you from?" Paolo asked through a mouthful of chicken. *This stuff tastes better than it smells,* he thought.

Doug laughed, "North Carolina. Charlotte, actually. Isn't everyone on a stock car team from North Carolina? Besides I hate to tell you what your West Coast accent sounds like to me. Where are you from?"

"Me?" said Paolo. "I'm from San Francisco. I was born there, but my folks emigrated from Portugal. My papa tells me I got a lot of different type of blood in me. He is Italian and my mama is from Armenia. How they got to Portugal, I'm not sure. The story changes and it has something to do with the war."

The conversation flowed as the two boys talked mostly about cars and racing. Paolo was elated to have someone in racing that could answer his questions. As it turned out, Doug's father worked for Orly Mann, and Doug had been attending stock car races as long as he could remember. He knew just about everybody in the sport, and those he didn't know he knew about.

Finally the talk turned to this weekend's event. Doug elaborated on the suspension problems they were having with the car. No one else seemed to have the same problems—broken spindles were a rarity. They were using the same parts as other teams and yet something was not quite right. Bear had carefully examined each component himself before bolting them together. The A arms had been scoped, which was a process that checked them for cracks, and each weld was painfully examined, but the problem persisted. Sometimes, but not always, a part in either the right front or left front suspension would give way, break the spindle, which was the part that held the brakes and wheel, and Orly would find himself out of control and in the wall. Prior to today the failures had been on oval tracks, and yet there seemed to be no rhyme nor reason for the failure. Bear was surprised to break one on a road course. Today's crash was the worst, and the whole team was going nuts trying to find the problem. In the last five races Orly had finished in the top ten only once, had crashed four cars, and was in danger of falling out of the hunt for the Winston Cup Championship. Besides that, everyone's nerves were getting pretty frazzled and the strain was beginning to show.

Doug scraped his plate with the plastic fork, picking up the last bit of coleslaw, ate a last fried potato, and commented, "Boy, that was pretty okay, but I haven't eaten that much grease since the drain plug fell out of my Chevy when I was changing the oil." Both boys laughed as they wiped the chicken grease from their chins.

"So what kind of Chevy you got?" asked Paolo with wide-eyed interest.

"Got a '69 Camaro that's as fast as a streak of lightning and turns in the twelve's in a quarter mile." Doug felt a pang of pain go through his chest when he mentioned his car. It was a project that he and his dad had worked on together and he was proud of it. They had put a lot of hours into the thing. The motor was awesome with lots of chrome and ran as clean as the wind. Together they had taken every little ding and scratch out of the body and then sprayed it a deep dark metallic green. Doug had hand rubbed and fine sanded every square inch of the painted surface in between each coat, taking out even the tiniest microscopic scratches. When they were finished, it shined like nobody's business. "How about you?"

"I got a Chevy too. A '64 Malibu. It's not like yours though, Doug. It's a beater with an old 327 and used to belong to Uncle Rollie. It's pretty clean, but it burns a little oil. I want to fix it up some. I'm working and trying to save some money to get a set of wheels for it. I'm not sure whether to go chrome or mags. What do you think?"

This question precipitated another conversation as the boys discussed the relative merits of various wheel manufacturers, which in turn led to engine components, gear ratios, camshafts, and manifolds. All too soon Uncle Rollie stuck his head out the back door and shouted, "Heya, Pally, come on. We gotta get moving. The lunch rush isa coming."

"I gotta go," said Paolo, sticking his hand out.

Doug took the hand and shook it warmly. "Thanks for the chicken. It was good to meet you. I gotta get going too." He turned his back and threw his leg over the scooter. He jumped on the kick starter five or six times before it started and gave Paolo a sheepish grin.

Paolo reached down and picked up the clipboard and watches and handed them to Doug. "Here, don't forget these."

Doug nodded thanks and headed toward the gate leading up the hill to the RV compound. He rode a little way, then stopped and turned around to face Paolo who was still standing looking at him.

"Hey, Paolo?" Doug shouted over the noise of the scooter.

"Yeah, Doug?"

"You want to come in the pits and watch qualifying with me from the top of the hauler?"

Paolo's grin spread the width of his face. "You mean it? Oh, man do I. You bet I do. Yeah, I mean, yes I do."

"Qualifying starts at 2:00. I'll come and get you around a quarter to. Get you into the pits. I hope we got something to run." With that Doug turned and rode up the hill.

Paolo threw open the back door of the Chicken Shack and raised his head with a quick prayer. "Thank you, Lord Jesus, for an answer to prayer. Forgive me for doubting you." Then he gave a loud whoop and went back to work. The chicken didn't smell quite as bad as it had before. Now all he needed was for Uncle Rollie to give him the time off. Please, Lord?

Uncle Rollie was agreeable. He had been young once and he loved Paolo very much. Besides, what good were uncles if they couldn't grant a wish for a favorite nephew now and then? By 1:30 Paolo found himself in the back of the Shack wiping things down, stacking crates and whatnot. Mercifully the lunch rush had died down a little and the rest of the crew could handle the business. Every thirty seconds he glanced at his watch. At twenty to two, he took off his apron and washed up in the sink, taking his time. He changed his shirt and tried to put some order in his wavy hair. Then he waited. He was struck by a thought and tried to sniff himself. *Man, I hope I don't smell too much like fried chicken.* As he went out the back door of the Shack, he casually glanced over to the side of the building opposite the pits. He was startled to meet the gaze of a man leaning against the wall, staring intently at him. The man wore a pair of large black sunglasses and a wide-brimmed hat that shaded his face. His chin was covered by a bushy beard, and he seemed oddly out of place at the racetrack. Paolo looked back at the man, and it seemed the man quickly averted his eyes and looked into the pits. Then he spun on his heel and walked off into the crowd.

Just about that time, Doug showed up with the scooter and motioned for Paolo to get on the back. The little machine huffed and puffed beneath the burden of the two teenagers as Doug waved his pass at the security guards and rode through the pit gate. Paolo gave them a wide smile and a wave as they went by.

In the meantime, Orly, Jimmy, and Bear sat in the lounge section of the transporter. Orly had his shirt off and was trying to adjust the ace bandage wrapped around his ribs. He was in obvious pain as he tried to move. "You want some help with that?" Bear asked.

"No," Orly snapped. "Hey, Bear, what in blue blazes is going on? This car was perfect. I mean right out of the box it was fast, and as soon as I get the thing up to speed and feel like I can trust it, we break a spindle. I tell you, Bear, in all my years of racin' I never broke a spindle without hitting something first. This is the fourth pickin' time this year we broke something in the front suspension, and that just don't happen. Am I right? You know I'm right." Orly was mad. He wasn't mad at Bear. He knew that if Bear had the solution he would fix it.

Orly went on, "I'm getting a little tired of this. Nobody else is having these problems. I can't see it having anything to do with down force, camber, or tires. The geometry on the front suspension is basically the same as everybody else. Besides we've been running this configuration

41

for a long time, and it is tried and true . . . and why are we having problems just now, anyway? I am getting plumb sick of this and besides it's getting really dangerous and starting to hurt." Orly's words ran together and he grunted as he wrenched the bandage a little tighter around his ribs.

"And on top of that, Bear, it costs us money. I hate it when we build a brand-new race car only to stuff it in the wall somewhere. It takes a lot of time and money to build these things." Orly went on.

Bear didn't say anything for a while. He knew Orly was frustrated, and anybody who just got pounded like Orly had had a right to be upset. Finally Bear spoke, "I know, Orly, I've been working on this full-time." He leaned against the wall with his hands deep in his pockets, his head down. "I can't figure it neither. I've talked to everybody I can, and none of the other guys are struggling with this. I've been over it a thousand times in my mind. I just can't figure it."

Jimmy interjected, "Are we buying all those parts from the same supplier?"

"No, some we buy from Chevrolet, some we buy from specialty manufacturers, and some we fabricate in the shop at home. At least we did until Bud Prescott took off," Bear responded. He bemoaned the fact that Prescott was gone; they needed him to help them get to the bottom of this problem. Bud was the best machinist that Bear had ever worked with, and he was also the fastest front tire changer in the world. The team especially missed him on race weekends. Bear was doing the front tire changing, but he wasn't nearly as fast as Bud. Bear shook his head.

"How much time are we going to have to practice with the spare car, Bear?" Orly asked, changing the subject.

"Not too much, but we'll get some laps in before qualifying takes place. I'm not sure how this car will handle, Orly, but we will be on top of it. It was built identical to the primary car, but you know how these things work," Bear responded.

Two cars could be built out of identical parts by the same people in the same shop and one would be fast and the other would simply be average.

"I think we will have enough time to get it half right. I built that front suspension myself. I've checked all the welds, and it is set up 'bout as good as it can be," Bear answered. *I also built the one that broke,* he thought.

"Yeah, I know, Bear. I just hope we can get the thing in the race. Let me take some aspirin for this headache and these ribs and rest a while."

Bear gave Orly a gentle slap on the back, gave a look to Jimmy, and then they headed out to help the crew stash the totaled primary car in the hauler and ready the backup car. As always there were a lot of media folks around, and Bear found himself giving quick interviews and putting the best spin that he could on the morning's events. Finally he cut things off with the explanation he had to help the crew get the car ready for the next practice session.

It would be a short one before the qualifying races. Teams drew lots to set the qualifying order, and every car and driver would have a chance to qualify by running one timed lap against the clock. The fastest qualifier got the first starting spot of the race, and also got a nice paycheck and a chance to participate in a special race for pole winners at the beginning of next year's season. It put a little extra incentive in the mix and kept things interesting for the fans. The rest of the field was arranged by how fast their times were around the track. On a typical race weekend the fastest twenty-five cars on Friday were guaranteed a spot in the race. The rest of the field could either take a chance and stand on their time or attempt to go faster on Saturday and move up in the field. Even if they went faster than Friday's qualifiers they could still start no better than twenty-fifth. The big problem was that the field was limited and there were always more cars than starting positions. Position was everything, especially at Sears Point where passing was exceedingly difficult on the narrow 1.9-mile course. With this reworked racetrack everything seemed difficult. Orly was scheduled to go out to qualify eighteenth.

Paolo was in the nearest thing to heaven. His neck was on ball bearings as he craned to see everything at once. He couldn't keep the silly grin off his face. Doug parked the scooter next to the hauler, out of the way. He gave Paolo a brightly colored piece of paper sheathed in plastic that said "Pit Pass," and then he said in a businesslike tone, "Here, put that on your belt. It's only good for today. I've got to talk to Bear for a minute. Take a walk around if you want, but don't bug the drivers for autographs right now. They're trying to get ready to qualify and everybody will be a little tense. Be back here in twenty minutes and we'll go topside."

Paolo nodded his head. As he walked his heart pounded. The pit garage was a busy place and just reeked of excitement. Right off, he recognized several drivers from the many times he had seen them interviewed on TV. The cars were all so fresh and bright looking and the crews looked sharp in their uniforms that matched the bright color schemes of the cars. Everybody that wore a uniform was busy doing something to the cars, even if it was just polishing. There were also a lot of men and women dressed in expensive clothes that looked slightly out of place. Paolo supposed they were the car owners or the sponsors who spent the millions of dollars to field a NASCAR team. There were also photographers and journalists and TV guys and cameramen all over the place. Every time a driver looked like he was halfway alone, he was besieged with people looking for autographs and pictures. Occasionally, Paolo would hear the deep-throated roar of a race car that sounded almost like a roar of a big animal as a crew started an engine to test for something. Periodically a car would rumble past on the way to the gas pumps to get just the right amount of fuel for qualifying. Paolo was forced to keep his wits about him as he wandered in the fenced garage area. He could see why the public was not allowed in here with all this activity going on.

As he casually walked by two haulers, he happened to glance down between them to the cyclone fence that enclosed the pits. There was that same man with the beard and the hat on the outside of the fence. He beckoned violently to Paolo. Paolo stopped, uncertain as to what to do. The man insistently waved at Paolo and motioned for him to come to the fence. Paolo looked around to make sure the man was waving at him and then pointed to his own chest. "Me?" he mouthed.

The man nodded vehemently and motioned once again. Paolo slowly worked his way between the two haulers and walked toward the fence. With all the thousands of people walking around inside and outside the pit area, it seemed very odd that a stranger would want to talk to him. He walked up to the fence. The man looked at him and poked two manila envelopes through the mesh. One seemed very thick and the two of them were held together with a rubber band.

"Take 'em," he said gruffly to Paolo. "Do what it says on them. Won't be any problem." The man motioned impatiently. "I was told not to say anything to Doug. It could hurt him," the man added with tight lips.

Paolo looked into the man's dark sunglasses and took the crumpled, sealed envelopes, feeling completely baffled. The thick one had written on the front the words, GIVE THIS TO THE CHAPLAIN!

On the other it said, GIVE THIS TO ORLY MANN.

As soon as Paolo took the envelopes, the man turned away and disappeared into the crowd. Paolo stood there, befuddled, uncertain just quite what to do. After a minute he turned and walked back the way he came.

"Hey! There you are, Paolo, how ya doing?" Paolo heard the familiar voice and turned around to face Doug.

A righteous man may have many troubles, but the LORD delivers him from them all; he protects all his bones, not one of them will be broken.

Psalm 34:19–20

"There's some people who come here to race and some guys that are racers. There's a difference. I'm lucky to be on a team with a bunch of great racers."

Randy LaJoie, Busch Series driver

TO THE UNEDUCATED, NASCAR qualifying seemed about as exciting as watching a freeway on-ramp on a slow day. Each car left the pit lane one at a time to attack the race-track by themselves with no other cars to slow them down or speed them up. They made a leisurely warm-up lap then came thundering by to pick up the green flag at the start-

47

finish line and drive around the racetrack as fast as they possibly could. Then the timed lap finished with the starter waving the checkered flag at the conclusion of the lap.

The times were then posted on the automated five-story timing tower for all to see and the rankings were either raised or lowered according to each car's qualifying time. The fastest car's time was posted at the top and the rest followed in accordance with their times. This went on until all of the cars trying to make the race had completed time trials. The fastest car then sat on what was called the "pole," which was the first starting spot of the race. A privilege that brought extra cash and other premiums as well as being the best place to start the race. Anybody that was passed in qualifying was somebody that wouldn't have to be passed in the race itself. Starting at the front or at least close to it carried prestige and notoriety. Race cars carried sponsor decals and logos for one purpose, and that was for the public to see and take notice. The closer to the front a car qualified, the more media attention it got. More media attention for the car and the driver meant more exposure for the sponsors. Sponsors liked exposure. It was what they paid for.

To the educated it was a far different scene. There were always more cars than starting positions for any given race. In order for a driver to earn points for a race he had to at least start it. It was a thirty-two lap schedule, and points were what decided championships. Points and finishing position also meant money, sometimes a lot of it. The pot for the winner this week was just a little over $160,000.00. And that was a lot of whatever money could buy by anybody's standards.

Getting into a race was never a given, and in the last few years competition had become so fierce that the time difference between the fastest of the fast who sat on the pole and the fortieth and final qualifier could be less than a second or two. Here at Sears Point starting position made a big difference. Passing was not easy on this twisty road course, and if a driver could start toward the front he had a better shot at winning the race or at least a good overall finish. Even tenth place still paid over $50,000.00. Besides that, nobody in the history of this race had ever won starting any farther back than thirteenth.

To qualify well a driver had to use every bit of his skill and a considerable amount of intestinal fortitude to make the car go as fast as it possibly could in a one-lap sprint. Even the setup for the car was different than for the actual race. A special engine was installed, designed to put out the most horsepower with little regard for how long it could run. It only had to last for two laps. These were often called "hand grenades"—pull the pin and put your foot down, and hope the thing didn't blow up before the qualifying lap ended. In the meantime, the driver had to hang on because the motor was going to give all it had . . . at least for a little while. The big race would be 112 laps and, with proper strategy and good fortune, could be completed with only three pit stops. But that all didn't matter right now. The important thing was to cut a hot lap and get in the race. After qualifying, the team could work on the race setup and tune for mileage and tire wear with the idea of building in some long-term reliability.

Orly and Bear were old hands with all of this. The practice laps with the backup car had proved two things. First, it wasn't nearly as fast as the primary car had been and second, Orly was in a lot more pain from the crash than he realized. It had taken a superhuman effort to muster the strength to lift his leg and step into the car for the practice session. Of course, the NASCAR official was right there watching him—he had the power to keep Orly off the track if he thought Orly wasn't ready physically to drive. So Orly smiled at him and made a lame joke about getting old as he fit himself through the driver's window in the classic style—right leg first, slide the hips, then the left leg while holding onto the roof with both hands. When he finally got himself inside and settled into the form-fitting driver's seat, he grunted with pain as he tightened the belts. He was hurting, but at least his head was clear. He'd had broken bone pain before and this wasn't it. It would subside after a while and by Sunday it wouldn't be a factor. That was if he could keep the car off the wall and on the track. Above it all Orly was a professional, and like many athletes he was able to put the pain aside as he and Bear went about the business of setting up the car for qualifying. The few laps went fast with Orly making comments over the radio about changes that needed to be made in the shocks and track bar. Maybe a little tire pressure adjustment might help some as well. Bear had done his best to have the car ready, but these cars were incredibly sensitive to variables like track temperature and weather conditions. Fine tuning was an art as well as a necessity. After the practice session there was a short break. The crews worked frantically on the cars, getting them ready to qualify.

Each car was parked behind the team's hauler and there was just enough room for the crews to work on the cars.

NASCAR parked the teams close together on purpose—rival teams kept each other honest. The rules were strict and every crew chief and team manager worth his considerable wages did everything they could to bend them to their own advantage. They were often seen examining each other's equipment. The three major automakers—Chevy, Ford, and Pontiac—had a lot at stake. Everyone in the sport knew that the car that won on Sunday more often than not sold good on Monday. And the more money for the big three, the more money for NASCAR. Money made the world go 'round, especially on the Winston Cup Circuit.

It was in this type of situation that Bear's ability as a crew chief really shone. A short time before qualifying, the race car had looked like some type of oversized puzzle with pieces scattered all over the place. It sat up on jackstands with the wheels off, looking unbalanced and ungainly. But Bear was in control. Inside his head ticked a subconscious clock, and he knew exactly how much time they had and how he was going to accomplish what needed to be done. The crew worked like a well-oiled machine. There was no time for conversation and only quick words were exchanged.

Bear was talking in a calm even voice with the tire man about air pressure settings, and as he finished that conversation he slid underneath the car to check with the chassis guys about track bar adjustments, shock travel, and varied suspension settings. When the chassis man reached for a wrench from the massive toolbox Bear had it in the man's hand without interrupting his conversation. Orly felt like the gear ratio needed a tooth to get better pull from the engine coming off the corners, so the rear end man had the driveshaft laying on the ground and was draining the oil in preparation for a gear change. In the meantime, the hood was up and two guys had their arms deep in the guts of the engine compartment as they adjusted throttle linkage, changed spark plugs, and checked for leaks. The carburetor was on the workbench in preparation for a jet change as another man was examining the old spark plugs through a magnifying glass, talking into Bear's ear while trying to get a read on fuel mixture. One crewman was inside the car, making adjustments to Orly's seat and the steering column in an effort to make him more comfortable. The fuel man was carefully measuring the precise amount of fuel it would take to qualify. No sense in putting too much in. It would only be extra, useless weight.

As Bear oversaw the work on the car he looked a lot like an ant in a sugar bowl. Occasionally Bear would sneak a glance at the front suspension, as if in an effort to somehow catch it making plans to fail once again. He was busy and efficient, but he wasn't happy. This suspension thing was just not right. It went against his ordered engineering sense. Things just did not fail of their own accord. There had to be a reason for things breaking. Stress loads or heat or . . . something. It troubled him and in his mind he had made the determination that he was going to get to the root of the problem. As soon as they got this car qualified he was going to find out why this was happening . . . period. Enough was enough.

Paolo had problems of his own. He had finally found himself where he wanted to be. It should have been the happiest day of his life in the culmination of his dreams. Here he was in the midst of the team colors and the organized chaos that was the fenced-in garage area of a genuine NASCAR stock car race. He was standing on top of Orly Mann's very own hauler next to a new friend, who knew all the ins and outs of professional racing, getting ready to watch qualifying for Sunday's race.

From his vantage point he could see any number of famous drivers and racing personalities. There was Ned Jarrett talking with Benny Parsons and Dr. Jerry Punch. The TNN and ESPN TV people and MRN radio celebrities were all over the place getting interviews and sound bytes. Paolo could almost taste the excitement in the pits. He should have been ecstatic but instead he was incredibly anxious and his stomach was turning cartwheels. The two envelopes in his right pants pocket felt like a hot brick. It seemed so unreal. A guy called to him, he walked over, the guy shoved two envelopes at him and insisted he take them. Told him not to tell Doug because it could jeopardize Doug's life, "hurt him" he said. Then he spun on his heel and disappeared into the crowd, leaving Paolo with his mouth open and about thirty unanswered questions. What should he do? Call the police? Should he tell Doug? The guy said not to. The guy said to do what it said on the envelopes. The thick one was supposed to go to the chaplain and the thin one was supposed to go to Orly Mann. He didn't even know who the chaplain was. What was he supposed to do? Walk up to Orly Mann and say, "Oh, by the way, some strange looking dude gave me this and said to give it to you"? This was Orly Mann he was talking about. Orly was his hero. One did not approach a hero without good reason. Paolo had watched Orly painfully crawl out of the race car after the practice session, and it didn't look like Orly would be in the mood to talk. Paolo breathed a silent prayer, "Lord, what should I do?"

The call went up for qualifying to begin. Before hitting the pit lane to qualify, the cars had to once again go through the "tech line" and be certified by the NASCAR officials that they were in compliance with the rules. Orly's crew with Bear's able leadership had quickly, but calmly, put the car back together and were pushing it toward the tech line. A couple of guys were still tightening fittings under the hood as they pushed it along, but the car was ready.

Doug got out his watches and opened up his clipboard and laid it out in front of him. He reached down and grabbed two sets of earphones and handed one to Paolo.

"Here, put these on. You'll be able to hear what I'm hearing. Usually Orly doesn't talk much, especially during qualifying. If I've got this channel list right we might be able to hear some of the other drivers, though."

Paolo couldn't keep the grin off his face as he placed the earphones over his ears. It almost made him forget about the envelopes in his pocket. At least for the minute.

🏁

Tech had been no problem, and Orly sat in the long line of brightly painted and decal-plastered cars waiting their turn to qualify. Bear was leaning in the window. He shoved the radio mouthpiece away from his lips and looked into Orly's face framed by his helmet and goggles.

"You okay, Orly?"

"Yeah, I think I'm okay, Bear. I'll be sore tonight but I think I'll be passable by Sunday." He grinned at Bear. "That's not a good term for a race car driver to use, is it?" Orly laughed a short chuckle. "We sure used up a lot of race car today, didn't we?"

Bear wasn't laughing. "That's what sponsors are for. Dog, Orly, I'm sorry. We have got to get to the bottom of this thing. I just cannot figure it out. There is something radical going on here. Somebody is messing with something. If we can qualify for the race today, then tomorrow I am taking apart that suspension down to the last possible piece. Then I'm going to hide the pieces under my bed and put it back together just before the race. There has got to be a rational explanation for all of this." Bear gently banged his head against the top of the car. He had the utmost respect for Orly and his capability as a driver, and it grieved him when he couldn't give him the best equipment, especially when Orly's well-being was at stake. Racing was tough enough without this.

"I got faith in you, Bear. We'll figure it out. In the meantime let's see if we can get this bucket of bolts into the show. I think I'm good for a couple of laps, and maybe this thing will stay together for us."

Their conversation was interrupted when a TV camera crew walked up with their microphones and wires.

The reporter, dressed like the drivers in a fireproof suit, faced the camera and said, "Orly Mann, after that terrific crash this morning, is sitting calmly in his Chevrolet, waiting his turn at qualifying. Let's see if we can get a word with him."

He then turned to Orly and asked, "Well, Orly, how are you feeling? Do you think you have a shot at the pole?" Then he shoved the microphone in Orly's face.

Orly smiled a relaxed grin and replied, "Well, Bob, anything is possible, I suppose. But realistically I don't think so. I'll be happy if we can just make the top twenty-five today so we don't have to try again tomorrow. Actually, I'll be real happy if we can just keep the shiny side up and keep it on the black part of the racetrack through this qualifying run. We haven't been real good at doing that lately."

Bear winced in silent agony, leaned over, and helped push the car down the pit lane as another car left the line and headed out onto the track. The camera crew walked alongside as the interview went on. Finally they finished and moved on to the next car in the line.

In the meantime Doug was busy. As cars headed out onto the track, Doug reached down and changed the channel selector on the radio unit strapped around his waist. This enabled him to eavesdrop on the other teams as they communicated back and forth with their drivers. Paolo stood next to him goggle-eyed with his hands on the earpieces as he silently listened. He was in another realm. This was amazing. A few hours ago he was up to his armpits in grease and dead chicken, and now he was a genuine member of a NASCAR crew with a genuine certified Motorola headset covering his ears and a pit pass on his belt. He was listening to some of his heroes share inside information with their crews about track conditions and whatnot. Not only that but he was privy to the general inside scoop about what was going on, and he was getting his information firsthand.

Man, how things changed, he thought, and then he suddenly felt the weight of the envelopes in the pocket of his jeans as he leaned against the rail of the observation platform. He closed his eyes and prayed quickly, "Please, Lord, answer my prayer and show me what to do."

Suddenly his brain hooked up as he watched a driver overcook it through the infamous "chute" into turn seven and a cloud of brown dust flew into the air. The car slid off the track backwards through the gravel pit and slammed lazily into the tire barrier. It was gentle as crashes went but it meant that the driver's try at qualifying was done for today and he would have to take another shot tomorrow.

Doug caught the action, quickly checked the chart in front of him, and dialed in his scanner. The radio chattered in Paolo's ear as the spotter, crew chief, and a much chagrined driver exchanged animated conversation.

Doug grinned at Paolo, lifted his earpiece, and yelled, "That's one we won't have to worry about. He'll have to try again tomorrow."

Paolo nodded his head in agreement.

Orly's crew pushed his car toward the beginning of the line. It was nearly time to see if they could put enough together to get in the race. Orly flipped the switches and pushed the starter button. The starter ground, but the engine didn't seem to want to catch. Orly checked the toggles that fired the electronics and glanced out the window to see Bear's concerned face staring back at him.

One of the crewmen handed Bear a spray can of ether. He leaned over and fired a blast of the volatile gas into the air scoop next to the windshield and pushed the transmit button at the same time. Bear spoke into his mouthpiece, "Try it again, Orly. Bill has got the timing so jacked on this thing it don't want to run." He was referring to Bill Bately, who built the motors for Orly's team.

Orly hit the button again and the motor slowly turned over, and then when it seemed as if the battery was going dead it suddenly caught with a deep bellow that settled into a steady stomach-churning rumble. Orly watched the gauges come up as he patiently waited his turn, doing his best to quiet his pounding heart. *That's all they need, a dead skunk on the qualifying line,* Orly thought.

Bear mopped his receding hairline with a shop rag and stuffed it in his back pocket.

Paolo and Doug's full attention was on Orly's car in the pit lane. They had a good view from their vantage point on top of the hauler and Doug gave Paolo a thumbs-up as Orly took his cue from the pit marshal and eased out onto the track.

For qualifying, a driver headed down what was normally the drag strip to warm up the car. It gave the driver time to warm the tires and get up to speed. Racing tires were designed to work best when they had a little heat in them. It made them stick better and gave the car better traction going in and coming off the corners. Then the driver could come charging down the back section of the racetrack, fly through turn eleven, and hit the start-finish line with a full head of steam to take the green flag flat out.

Orly took his time warming the car, holding it in third gear to get things loosened up. He kept his foot on the brake pedal, heating up the brake pads and rotors. They too worked best with a little heat. As he passed through turn seven he began to pick up momentum and dialed in his concentration so that every fiber of his being was in tune with what was happening with the car. He didn't bother to acknowledge the click of the radio as he passed by Jimmy. As he came down the esses he picked up speed and smoothly passed through the very quick turn ten at about 70 percent of full race speed. His mind wandered a minute when he passed over the ugly black skid marks from this morning's crash, but he quickly snapped back into focus. He settled back in the seat, shifted gears, and powered out of turn eleven just brushing the pit wall as he set the car up for the green flag.

He was serious as he flashed by the start-finish line, and the flag man vigorously waved the green flag. Orly chose his line carefully through turn one, trying to be as absolutely smooth as he could. This was a deceptive left-hander that required precision. Did no good to throw the car around in fancy slides. It might look spectacular, but as the tires lost adhesion they created friction and slowed the car down in the corners. The goal was to keep as much power on the ground as long as possible. Orly called on his years of experience and familiarity with the Sears Point circuit. He liked this place and drove it well. He was through one and up the hill and into turn two without a bobble. He felt a little push going into three and had to back off just a tick. It would cost him time but it was better to complete the lap than pick wildflowers in the field. The corners unfolded and his concentration was so intense it seemed as if before he had started he was back in turn ten. This time, however, he was as smooth as glass, hitting the apex of the corner perfectly. Then he was in turn eleven, through it, and flashing in front of the starter stand to pick up the checkered flag. He knew in his bones that this lap was not an exceptionally fast time, but he had gotten all the car had to offer. He hoped it was good enough.

"How'd we do, Doug?" Orly asked.

Bear looked down at his watch, biting his lip. *Oh, well,* he thought. If they had to qualify tomorrow it would give them more time to tune the car. Bear was certain it had a lot left in it. They just hadn't had time to find it yet. He made a face and groaned. *Man, I hope we don't have to do that. We need some time to sort out this suspension thing.*

"We're eighteenth, Orly, right where we started, but there are still a lot of guys left to go. Some of them were pretty quick in practice so . . . well, I'm not sure," Doug said.

"Hey, Bear," Orly said. "Even if we don't make the show today I think we can tune enough to make the show with this thing tomorrow."

Qualifying dragged on, and gradually Orly dropped from eighteenth to nineteenth then to twentieth. Twenty-fifth was the cutoff point. Orly had climbed out of the car, and much to Paolo's delight, climbed up on the hauler to stand behind Doug and him so he could watch the watches. He didn't say much but Paolo could tell he was nervous and trying not to show it. Paolo kept sneaking looks at him out of the corner of his eye. He was bigger than he seemed on TV.

With only a few cars left, Orly had been bumped down to twenty-third and the conversation on the roof of the hauler dwindled. There were four cars left to qualify. Then there were three and Orly was twenty-fourth. The number held as the last three drivers did everything they could to make the race but fell hundredths of a second short.

When the last car took the checkered flag and the watches were compared, the official order of qualification came over the loudspeaker. Doug let out a whoop and slapped Paolo on the back, turned around and slapped Orly on the shoulder. Orly winced but returned Doug's smile.

Doug turned to Paolo and pounded his back. "We did it, Paolo. We are in and we can concentrate on the race setup. Oh, boy, what a relief."

Orly tousled Doug's hair and said, "Hey, Dougie, who's your friend? I don't think you have introduced me yet."

"I'm sorry, Orly. This is Paolo Pellegrini. He's a fan of yours from way back." Doug winked at Paolo. "I invited him up here to watch qualifying with us. He's a good guy."

Paolo blushed and completely lost his cool as he grinned stupidly and shook Orly's outstretched hand. Then he felt the weight of the envelopes in his pocket and swallowed real hard. *How am I going to do this?* he thought.

"Nice to meet you, Paolo. Be seeing you again, I suspect." Orly smiled, then climbed down the ladder and was gone. Doug followed. Paolo wanted to kick himself for losing the opportunity to talk directly to Orly and maybe give him the envelope. He was just too embarrassed to do it.

The roof of the hauler had been an oasis in the midst of chaotic activity. The garage area now resembled a carnival midway. The only thing missing was the Ferris wheel. Hundreds of folks were milling around, trying to get autographs and interviews. Most of the drivers retreated to the lounge areas of their haulers. There was a huge mob around the hauler of the team that had won the pole position for the race. The driver was being interviewed with at least ten microphones stuck in his face, and he was having to repeat his comments several times to be understood.

In the meantime, the crews were trying to pack up equipment and tools and bed down the race cars in the haulers for the night. Paolo found himself standing with Doug next to the back of the big truck in the midst of all the activity when a middle-aged, powerfully built man walked up behind Doug and lifted him off the ground in a big hug.

"Hello, Doug, how you doing? I see you guys made the show today."

The tone of the man's voice was sincere, and he had an easy gentleness about him as he set Doug back on the ground. One had the feeling that he really was interested in how Doug was doing and his horseplay was just a way of making contact. Doug seemed to relax under the man's embrace and the tenseness went out of his face for a moment.

"I'm doing okay, Pastor John. Yup, we're in. After this morning we needed a break, and Orly and Bear put it all together pretty good. I want you to meet my friend Paolo."

Pastor John, Pastor John! This is the guy, thought Paolo. *This is the chaplain! This is the man who is supposed to get one of the envelopes.* He resisted the temptation to take the envelope out of his pocket like a hot coal and fling it at the smiling man. *Must be the same guy,* he thought. *I'm not going to miss my chance again. I can't.*

"Hi, Pastor John, my name is Paolo Pellegrini. Pleased to meet you." Paolo stuck out his hand.

John took it, looked him in the eye, and smiled warmly. Paolo liked this man immediately. He seemed like someone who could be trusted.

"Hello, Paolo. Nice to meet you. Didn't I see you and Doug at the back of the Chicken Shack earlier this afternoon?"

"Yeah, my Uncle Rollie owns the franchise and I'm helping him out. Then I met Doug and I got to come in here and watch qualifying . . . and well, here I am." Paolo shrugged with an open-handed gesture. Doug had slipped into the hauler to put away the watches and radio equipment, leaving Paolo and Pastor John talking.

Paolo gulped, made his decision, and went for it. "Pastor John, can I talk to you for a minute?"

"Sure, Paolo." Pastor John put his arm around Paolo's shoulder and gently guided him between two haulers for a modicum of privacy in the midst of the crowd of people.

Paolo poured out the story in a rush of words and concluded it by pulling out the thick envelope, leaving the one for Orly still in his pocket. He glanced at the front of it and then thrust it into Pastor John's hand. Pastor John furrowed his brow as he took the envelope.

"Now wait a minute, Paolo, slow down. The man said that you were to give this to me? Did he say anything else?"

"Yes, ah, I mean no. I mean he said I wasn't to talk to anybody about anything or, uh, he just said give it to you, that's all. So I can't say any more," Paolo concluded with an agonized look on his face. He knew he shouldn't say any more. The stranger had told him Doug could be hurt.

John looked intently at him as if he knew Paolo wasn't telling him everything.

About that time, Doug came out of the hauler and climbed onto the scooter. He kicked it several times before it finally started with a cloud of smoke. Then he rode over to where Paolo and Pastor John were talking and gave Paolo a wave.

"Come on, Paolo, I'll give you a ride back to the Chicken Shack."

Relieved that he saw Doug, Paolo gave Pastor John a wave and a weak smile, turned, and climbed on the back of the scooter. *I should have told him the rest,* Paolo thought.

Pastor John gave Paolo and Doug a wave back. With a puzzled look on his face, he casually hefted the envelope in his hand and studied the writing on the front of it. He didn't recognize it. The envelope was heavy and thick. Finally he reached in his pocket, pulled out a penknife, and slit the flap of the envelope. Inside was a thick sheaf of hundred dollar bills with a small white card. Typed on the card in bold print were the words, PLEASE GIVE THIS TO THE PRESCOTT FAMILY.

He studied the card while it was still in the envelope, then looked at the thick wad of bills. He let out a small whistle between his lower teeth. He estimated that there were several thousand dollars there.

Bear and the crew were getting ready to push the car onto the hydraulic lift that would raise it to the storage platform in the hauler. As Bear walked in front of the car, he happened to look at the right front wheel. He stopped suddenly and sank down on his haunches. The tire was sitting at just the tiniest of an unnatural angle. To Bear's trained eye it meant only one thing. The right front suspension had just about been ready to break when Orly pulled off the track. One more lap would probably have ended in disaster like this morning. His knees gave out and he fell back on his rear end with both hands on his head.

Do not be anxious about anything, but in everything, by prayer and petition, with thanksgiving, present your requests to God.

Philippians 4:6

"I didn't realize at first how hard it was to win a race, and I'm not sure I realized how much it cost. But it has been about as exciting as anything I have ever been part of."
Joe Gibbs, former Washington Redskins coach and Super-bowl winner. Owner of the Interstate Batteries Pontiac, driven by Bobby Labonte (car #18) and the Home Depot Pontiac driven by rookie Tony Stewart (car #20)

PAOLO CLIMBED OFF the scooter at the back door of the Chicken Shack. He looked at the empty crates stacked around the big outdoor refrigerator, shrugged his shoulders, and turned back to Doug.

"Hey, Doug, thanks for the invite and everything. I can't believe I actually watched qualifying from the pits and met Orly Mann and . . . well it was pretty . . . well thanks," Paolo stammered. "I better get in there and help clean up. Uncle Rollie said he was going to teach me how to clean the Acme-Jiffy-Deep-Fat-Fryer." Paolo said this with pauses in between each word, making it sound like a major technological operation. "I can hardly wait."

Doug laughed out loud at his new friend's hangdog look and his obvious lack of enthusiasm. "Man, I don't blame you, Paolo. It sure don't sound like fun to me."

Paolo changed the subject. "Hey, Doug, what do you do now? I mean, NASCAR locks up the garage area at five o'clock, don't they?" Paolo was referring to the NASCAR policy of locking the gates to the garage area at night and not allowing any team to work on their cars. They would open them back up at 7 A.M. the next morning. It was part of keeping everyone on the same page in regard to the rules. Precisely at 5 P.M. the NASCAR officials would come through the area like a teacher pushing kids off the playground after recess. Everyone would be herded out the gate and the place would be secured with a lock and security personnel.

"What are you doing tonight?" Paolo was beginning to hatch a plan in his mind. He still had to get that envelope to Orly. He felt tremendously relieved to be done with the other envelope. That one was Chaplain John's problem now.

I wonder what was in it—that other one? Paolo thought. It sure was heavy. Now if he could just get rid of this one. Without Doug that would be impossible. Anyway, if Doug was with him maybe he would be safer. Besides that, he thought again, he really liked Doug and even though they had only met today it was as if they had been friends for a long time. It was exciting and fun to be with Doug. He knew all those celebrities that Paolo had only just read about.

Now it was Doug's turn to look glum. "Oh, I'll head back to the motor home and probably have a little supper with Bear and a couple of the crew. Probably watch some TV. We got the satellite dish, you know, then I'll go to bed. Pretty boring actually." The thought of an empty evening and sleeping in the motor home, coping with Bear's snoring, was suddenly less than appealing. That guy could shake the dishes in the cupboards and rattle the blinds against the windows.

"Doug, listen. I've got an idea. Why don't you come home with me and spend the night? I have an extra bed in my room. You'll like my folks. Tonight is when the youth group at my church meets, and you could come. Then afterwards I'll show you San Francisco. You never been there, have you?"

"Well, not really. At least not long enough to do any sightseeing."

"Everybody ought to see the city, sometime, especially at night. Come on, what do you say? I have to be here early tomorrow, like you, so I could bring you back, no sweat."

"I dunno, Paolo. It sounds kind of fun, but I'd have to check with Orly and Bear. They sort of keep an eye on me for my mom. They don't really, I mean. Everybody trusts me I guess. I guess I could. Let me check with them. I would like to see San Francisco." Doug threw his leg over the scooter. "I'll be back in a little while. What time you gonna be done cleaning up?"

Orly and Bear were okay with Doug going. They knew that life on the road with a race team was a lot less glamorous than folks suspected, especially for an eighteen-year-old who acted like he was thirty-five. Everyone on the crew worked so hard that partying was usually not an option. The day started early and every crewman was expected to be dressed and looking sharp when the gate opened to the garage area. The activity was nonstop, and sometimes by the end of the day the crew had taken the car apart and put it back together several times. One of the things that made a race successful was attention to the smallest details. Mistakes were made when team members were suffering from lack of sleep and too much partying.

It used to be that everybody stayed in motels and hotels, but now many of the crews stayed right at the track to save driving time and expense. Most NASCAR races were sold-out affairs, and trying to get to and from the racetrack was a real struggle, especially on race day. The traffic could be ferocious and some of the backups at various tracks were legendary. Sears Point was no exception and Highway 37 and 121 would be tough. The drivers that stayed in hotels usually flew back and forth to the track in rented or leased helicopters. It cost money but it sure was a lot easier. The crews, on the other hand, needed to spend every minute they could massaging the race cars for the race, and time sitting in traffic was time wasted.

After a hard day in the garage area many crew members relaxed in the evenings by sitting in front of their motor homes telling stories and giving each other a bad time. The motor homes were state of the art with showers and good beds. Some teams even brought their own cooks to prepare good nourishing food as opposed to the usual greasy burgers and deep-fried racetrack fare.

Those drivers who didn't stay in hotels had their own motor homes driven to the track by crew members who followed the brightly colored haulers back and forth across the country. They stayed in their own section of the compound. Many drivers were family men, and when it was convenient the driver and his family would fly in their private or corporate planes to whatever track they were racing at and camp out in luxury with satellite dishes, computers, and all the latest in technological toys. In some respects it was like a traveling circus.

In this way life was easier to control for everyone. With the popularity of stock car racing, many drivers generated the same excitement as if they were movie stars. They couldn't get through a meal in a public place or walk down the street without being bothered for interviews or autographs. All of the drivers had killer schedules, trying to keep sponsors, team owners, and media people happy. They made big money but big money brought big responsibilities. The days of just climbing inside a race car and making it go fast were long gone. A driver had to have personality and be able to sell the product that paid the bills for the team owners.

As a result, family time was a precious commodity. It had long been determined that the motor home compound for the racing folks was to be a safe haven and as a result off-limits to the public and the press. Security was tight and the drivers and their families were happy for the privacy.

70

With the busy racing schedules the outside view from the motor homes might change but usually the faces didn't. Chaplain John and his wife, Martha, had a lot to do with keeping a family atmosphere around the compound, and the wives appreciated it. They were available to anyone, and many counseling and prayer sessions had taken place around the table of their older motor home.

Chaplain John was the pastor of an unusual mobile church. Not everyone in the compound was a part of it, and there were those who scoffed and made fun of it. Those who were part of it appreciated John and his wife and loved and respected them very much. John often joked about having the fastest moving congregation in the world, especially on race day.

They led Bible studies at night for various groups and always had Sunday school for the kids and a chapel service for the families and crews early on Saturday evening. Chaplain John and Martha were close by and available for counsel, and they were quick to respond if anyone got hurt or needed help. On many occasions they spent long hours sitting at hospitals with friends and families for the inevitable racing injuries. Chaplain John had officiated at a number of funerals and memorial services in the passing of members of this unique fraternity. He had also had the pleasure of taking part in the marriage ceremonies of many folks as well.

🏁

Paolo came out of the back of the Chicken Shack with the reek of grease mixed with industrial strength cleanser hanging off him like an ill-fitting suit. He was pleasantly surprised to see Doug sitting on a crate, dressed in street clothes with an athletic bag in Orly Mann team colors at his feet.

"You finally done?" he asked with a gentle grin. "You get that fryer to pass inspection?"

"Man, let's get out of here. I need some air. If I don't get out of this place pretty soon I'm going to be sick. Just the smell of grease makes me gag." Paolo screwed his features into a gruesome face and made poking motions down his throat.

Doug laughed out loud and said, "Excuse me, Paolo, do you mind walking downwind a little? You smell kind of ripe. Is that a feather I see growing out of your ear there?" With that both boys laughed.

They walked over to the parking lot to Paolo's car, and as he fumbled in his pocket for the keys, Doug surveyed the old but classic Chevy. It needed work but it was clean and polished, and he could tell that Paolo took pride in it. They climbed in and Paolo started the engine. It caught on the first try and idled like a contented, well-fed cat.

"Hey, Paolo, not bad. You got enough gas?" Doug commented. Then he paused with a funny look on his face. "Don't know why I said that. It's just something my dad always said to me when he got in my car. Habit I guess."

Paolo glanced over and said nothing, sensing that perhaps Doug needed to talk. As Paolo concentrated on his driving, Doug continued to ramble. He explained to Paolo how his dad had just suddenly disappeared one night and how painful it was not knowing where he was. He was very worried about him. His mom seemed almost unconcerned about it, saying, "Your father will be back before long. If he could tell you why he had to go you know he would—just be patient." But Doug couldn't seem to accept her explanation. He was obviously missing him and he said his sister was having a hard time. She was a lot younger than Doug and missed her "sweet Daddy," as she called him. His name was Bud and he was the best and the fastest front tire changer in all of stock car racing. Many teams had tried to hire him away from Orly, but Bud was loyal to the team. He had known Bear and Orly for a long time. He also was the best machinist in the world and worked long hours at Orly's shop at home. Whenever there was a problem of some sort Bear relied a lot on him.

Paolo simply listened, making encouraging comments that kept Doug talking. It was obvious that Doug had a lot of stuff bottled up and not much opportunity to let it out. He could tell that Doug loved his dad, and Paolo was content to let him talk.

As Paolo's old Chevy purred down 101 North toward San Francisco, Doug found himself relaxing. He liked Paolo very much, and it was great joy for him to have someone his own age to talk to. Paolo was easygoing and nonjudgmental and he laughed easily. Like Doug he was also mature and was used to taking care of himself, and yet Doug could tell he had deep respect for his parents too. Paolo seemed to ask just the right questions and made the right comments that made him feel comfortable telling his story. Somehow talking seemed to ease the pain a little and he felt his gloominess dissipating.

It was one of those unusual crystal clear evenings when they descended the Waldo grade to cross the Golden Gate

Bridge. Summertime usually meant that the fog would roll in early in the evening, but not tonight. The bright sun was just beginning to quench itself in the darkness of the Pacific Ocean.

To Doug's delight Paolo pulled off at the south end observation area and parked the car. They got out and walked the ramp that led out onto the bridge itself. Doug's head was on a swivel as he tried to see the city and the bay on one side and the broad expanse of the ocean on the other.

Paolo laughed when Doug stopped and said, "Man, this thing moves around, doesn't it? I can feel it bounce up and down."

"You bet it does. It's a suspension bridge and it sways quite a bit. You ought to stand out in the middle on a windy day," Paolo replied.

They walked out on the walkway next to the traffic lanes, and Doug peered over the edge of the railing. "Oh man, Paolo, but that is a long way down there and that water looks mighty cold and fast. I bet those waves are bigger than you think, huh?" He continued, "Sure seems weird to see the sun go down in the ocean. In Carolina it rises from the ocean." Doug rattled on, "Boy, look at that city and how tiny those sailboats look. Now what is that little island right there? Why I'll bet that is—"

"Yup, there is Alcatraz and Angel Island. And if you look this way real carefully you can see Japan," said Paolo.

Doug turned around to look and then lightly punched Paolo's shoulder. "You are teasin' me." He laughed.

"No, really, if you look real close . . . okay you can't see it because of the curve of the earth. But it is out there somewhere. Actually those little islands are called the Faralones and there are a lot of great white sharks out there. No kidding. Come on, we've got to go. Mom will have dinner ready for us."

Getting back in Paolo's car, they crossed the bridge, and Paolo took the Nineteenth Avenue off-ramp. He lived out in the avenue section of the city, in the Sunset District. Paolo and his family lived in a typical San Francisco two-story flat that sat cheek to cheek with its neighbor. There was no front yard, only concrete, and the entrance was up a flight of concrete stairs.

The boys got out of the car, and Paolo's mom greeted them as they came upstairs. Paolo was the youngest of five children, and his brothers and sisters had all moved out of the house into their own places. Mrs. Pellegrini was a pleasant lady who clucked and talked nonstop. Doug could see where Paolo got his curly dark hair and propensity toward plumpness.

Paolo introduced Doug just about the time his dad came up from the postage-stamp backyard. He had been putzing in his little garden and had a handful of fresh lettuce and radishes for supper. He was a relaxed man somewhere in his late fifties with a gentle twinkle in his eye, and Doug could tell he was used to young people. Liked them very much in fact. He shook Doug's hand and welcomed him warmly to their house. "North Carolina, huh. Boy, you are a long way from home. Make yourself comfortable. We're glad to have you. We'll have supper directly."

"You boys wash up and get ready for supper," Mrs. Pellegrini said. "You better get a move on if you are going to make the youth group tonight, Pally. Oh, by the way,

Pally, I cooked your favorite for dinner. Fried chicken!" Then she chuckled out loud as Paolo groaned going up the stairs.

Doug made small talk with the Pellegrinis while Paolo was upstairs showering.

While changing clothes after his shower Paolo placed the remaining envelope marked "Orly Mann" on his dresser. It stared at him mutely as he combed his hair. He thought about leaving it, just forgetting the whole thing, but he grabbed it back up and put it in his pocket as he left his room.

Paolo's mom had only been kidding—dinner was actually a wonderful pasta with a sauce that beat anything that Doug would have eaten in the motor home. And there was plenty of that San Francisco sourdough French bread that crackled and melted in his mouth. The four of them ate at a little table in the kitchen, and the conversation was quick and lively. Paolo told his folks all about his day and watching qualifying from the top of the hauler. Neither one of his parents understood much about racing, but they were grateful that Doug had been nice to their son. Paolo's dad remarked, "It was nice of Rollie to give you the time off, Pally."

"Yeah, Pop, it was nice of him. I told him too and thanked him," Paolo replied.

With the warmth of the company Doug found himself fighting off pangs of homesickness for his own mom and sister. Ah well, he would be home Monday. *I wonder if there is any word from Dad,* he thought. *No there isn't.* If there was, Mom or Bear would call him and let him know right away.

The boys pushed back from the table, and Paolo gave his mom a quick kiss and his dad a hug and headed out the door.

"Come on, Doug, we're going to be late. Let's go."

"I've got the spare bed made up for you in Paolo's room, Doug. You'll be fine. And there is a clean towel for you in the bathroom," Paolo's mom said as the boys bounced down the stairs to the street.

Doug acknowledged with a wave of thanks and followed Paolo.

The church building was old but it was alive. The youth group met in the basement in a large room that smelled a little musty but had walls plastered with posters and snapshots. The noise was just under bedlam as about forty to fifty kids chattered and filled the air with laughter and horseplay.

Pastor Tom was the leader of this group. His official title was Pastor of Student Ministries, but he was happier with just being called Tom by the kids. He was standing in front of the room, surrounded by five or six young people all talking at once, when he spotted Paolo and Doug.

"Hey, Paolo, how ya doing? Who's your friend?"

Paolo introduced Doug and told him about some of the events of the day.

"It was so cool to be in the pits with him today," Paolo said.

Doug blushed a little and said nothing. He noticed right off that this was an unusual group—there were kids here of all colors, shapes, and sizes. African-Americans, Hispanics, Asians, and some kids that could be Indian or Polynesian even. Some had multicolored hair in different shades of red, orange, and purple. He also noticed that a number of kids were tuning guitars and getting a keyboard set up and adjusting a set of drums, getting ready to do some serious playing.

Finally Tom called the group to order and the young people grabbed chairs or flopped on cushions scattered around the room.

"Before we get started with the music, I see that we have a number of visitors with us tonight. How about some introductions?" said Tom.

Various people stood up and introduced their guests. When it was Paolo's turn, he said in a mock ringmaster's voice, "This is my friend Doug Prescott. He's from North Carolina, and he's out here with the world-famous Orly Mann Racing Team, which is competing at the world-famous Sears Point International Raceway located at the gateway to the prestigious Napa Valley—"

"North Carolina," Paolo was interrupted. "Is he one of them 'good ol' boys' we all hear about?" said an African-American young man from his position on the floor, drawing out the "we all" with a southern twang. It brought forth a nervous giggle from the group.

Paolo's eyes flashed. "Hey, Alphonse, lighten up. You know we don't talk that way. All of us in this room are children of the Lord Jesus Christ. It doesn't matter where we are from, how we talk, or what we look like."

Alphonse looked down for a minute, then looked back up at Doug.

"You're right, Paolo. I'm sorry, Doug. Didn't mean anything by it. Glad to have you with us."

Doug smiled back. "Yeah, no offense taken. No, I'm no redneck, but I might be considered a Tar Heel, I guess. I'm glad to be here, but I have to admit that you California folks do things different. And you sure do talk funny," he said, doing everything he could to broaden his North Carolina accent. This brought a genuine laugh from the group.

As Doug started to sit back down on the floor, a slim Asian girl slipped between him and Paolo. She sat down and nimbly crossed her legs, looked first at Paolo and said, "Hi, Pally," then turned and smiled at Doug and said, "Hi. I'm Alicia Chen. Welcome to California. I'm always late, and Pally doesn't like it." Doug smiled back shyly, saying nothing as he looked over her head to a scowling Paolo and scooting over to make room for her.

The music was lively and it set the tone for worship as the young people sang and prayed together. It wasn't long before Doug felt at home and accepted. He found himself truly ready to listen as Tom stood up with his Bible to teach the message of the evening.

Paolo, on the other hand, was preoccupied. He couldn't stay focused during the worship time. His mind kept slipping back to the envelope in his pocket and what he should do about it. Finally, when he couldn't stand it any longer he closed his eyes and prayed, *"Lord Jesus, I don't know what to do. I just commit this to you. You show me what my next step is and I'll take it."*

Tom opened his Bible and read out loud,

A man of many companions may come to ruin,
but there is a friend who sticks closer than a brother.

"This passage is found in the Book of Proverbs in chapter 18, verse 24. Who is the friend that sticks closer than a brother?"

"Jesus!" shouted several members of the group.

"Why does he stick close to us?" Tom asked.

"Because he loves us," the group responded.

Then Tom read the final words of Jesus in the Gospel of Matthew and concluded with, "And surely I am with you always, to the very end of the age."

The following discussion covered not only how Jesus could be a true friend but also the responsibility of those who called him Lord to be an example of his love to each other.

Tom's teaching style was gentle as he allowed the young people to interact with each other in discussion, doing his best to guide their lively conversation.

It was Alicia Chen who brought things to a head as she commented, "You know, I think the greatest responsibility we have to each other as Christians is to be honest with each other. When we are honest with each other then the next thing we have to do is to give each other room to be different. You know what I mean? Room to change. We don't do that very often. I guess we put people in boxes and then never let them out. I know people do that to me, and I do it to other people too."

Doug seemed to be listening intently, saying nothing. Paolo was rapidly coming to a decision about what to do with the envelope and barely heard what was going on. His thoughts were finally beginning to sort them-selves out.

The meeting ended in an extended time of prayer. Tom asked for requests and several young people responded with concerns. Doug had a lump in his throat as Alphonse spoke out in a low voice, with his head bowed.

"I wish you guys would pray for me and my mom and sisters. Since my father left us it hasn't been easy. Maybe you could pray that God might bring him back. I miss him a lot."

Finally Doug found the courage to speak. "Uh, maybe I could ask you guys to pray for me and my family. Uh, my dad left us too and, Alphonse, I guess I know a little of what it feels like. Sorry, man."

Alphonse gave Doug a wave of acknowledgment as the group bowed their heads and began to pray. After the prayer time the band cut loose, filling the place with lively wall-banging music.

As the group began to break up, Paolo's eyes met Doug's and he jerked his head toward the door signaling that it was time to go. Alphonse came across the room and stuck out his hand. "Hey, man, didn't mean to offend you. Me and my family had a bad experience in the south one time when I was a little kid. Sometimes my mouth gets me in trouble. Sorry. Sorry to hear about your dad too. I've decided that when and if I'm ever a dad I'm going to stick it out no matter what."

Doug took his hand and said, "Yeah, me too. Thanks, man. Take care. Maybe I'll see you again sometime."

Alicia tucked herself between Paolo and Doug as they headed out the door.

"Where you guys going, Pally?" she asked.

"I'm going to show Doug around the city, you know, the usual sights."

"Can I come? We can take him to my Aunty Grandmother's restaurant in Chinatown; I'm sure he'll like that. Come on, Doug. You'll have a good time." She grabbed Doug's arm and headed toward Paolo's car. Paolo threw his hands up in disgust and followed after.

Paolo was upset. Alicia wasn't part of his plan. Oh, he liked her. He liked her a lot, as a matter of fact. She was fun to be with, and he could usually talk to her about a lot of things and she would listen. They had been friends most of their lives. Their parents were friends, and Paolo and Alicia had grown up in the church together. But lately she had changed. She was a lot harder to get along with. She had her own ideas about how things should be done and what Paolo should be doing. It was a tough thing for Paolo to get used to. She had also been looking at him differently—occasionally he would find her staring at him. Quite frankly it unnerved him.

At any rate it was useless to argue with her, so he simply got in the car and drove.

The evening had deepened into a very clear night, which was unusual for this time of year. The city was alive and filled with tourists as the three young people hit the familiar landmarks of San Francisco. Paolo took them to the top of Telegraph Hill, and they sat on the bricks around Coit Tower and watched the bay below them. Alicia and Paolo were old hands at showing off the beauty of San Francisco and the surrounding area, and Doug found himself entranced by their descriptions and friendliness. Seeing things from a teenage perspective made it even more fun for Doug. Bear and Orly were okay, but they weren't kids anymore. They took everything so serious. He found himself laughing at the same things that Paolo and Alicia laughed at and taking pleasure at the inside jokes and raised eyebrows they shared with one another.

Later on, Paolo parked the car and they hopped a cable car that clanged and rattled over the steep San Francisco hills. Doug was enthralled and just a little nervous as the ancient machine groaned its way to the top of yet another steep grade when Alicia and Paolo suddenly jumped off before it had stopped completely and beckoned him to follow. When he did they grabbed him under the arms and walked down the street singing at the top of their lungs, "We're off to see the Aunty Grandmother" to the tune of "We're Off to See the Wizard."

Two blocks later they were in the midst of a different culture and community as the bright lights and smells of Chinatown assailed Doug's senses. Paolo and Alicia headed down a little alley off the main street. A quick step through a lighted doorway and they were in a busy dining room full of people noisily eating a variety of exotic Chinese dishes. Waiters were running full tilt back and forth across the room, carrying immense trays of wonderfully aromatic food. It was a place of bustling activity, and presiding over it all was an ancient Chinese lady who sat on a stool in the corner behind the cash register coolly surveying the activity.

She spotted the young people coming through the door and directed a long-winded stream of Chinese to

Alicia. Alicia laughed and spoke back in Chinese and then gave the old woman a quick hug and kiss on the cheek. Paolo and Doug simply smiled. The old woman looked Paolo in the eye and then quickly pinched his cheek and said something to him in Chinese. He forced a smile as Alicia grabbed his arm and dragged him and Doug through a kitchen that seemed twice as busy and noisy as the dining room. Doug caught a quick glimpse of what looked like a whole army of cooks, stirring woks and pots creating great clouds of steam and smoke that was sucked into a fan above an immense stove. Waiters wove in and out as they picked up plates and bowls like halfbacks following their blockers. The place was noisy, and it seemed that everyone was shouting at the top of their lungs. Alicia led them into a small room in the back. It was quieter here, and they sat down around a small table.

Before they could get settled, a waiter placed silverware and chopsticks on the table, a pot of tea in front of them, accompanied by three Cokes. He engaged in a quick conversation in Chinese with Alicia. She smiled, rattled off an answer that took several seconds and then the waiter was gone.

Alicia smiled at Doug and said, "Betcha you never been in a place like this before Tar Heel boy."

"Uh, you got that right. Is that lady your aunt or your grandmother? Does she own this place?" Doug asked.

"She is both, and it is a long story. And in case you're wondering, she chewed me out for not coming around more often. She gets on me, and says she thinks sometimes I forget I'm Chinese. I don't, but she gets after me anyway. Wants me to learn the old ways and all that." Alicia turned and looked at Paolo. "She said you are looking good, Pally. She thinks you have put on some weight, but she likes you."

"I wish she wouldn't pinch my cheek. She does that every time she sees me. She's done that to me practically my whole life." Paolo rubbed his cheek as he spoke.

In practically no time at all the waiter was back with the food. Mama Pelligrini's supper had worn off, and Doug found himself surprisingly hungry. The Chinese food was hot, fresh, and super good. Alicia gave Doug a running commentary about what was what as she filled his plate. Then she carefully instructed him in the use of the chopsticks and laughed uproariously at his ineptness.

"I'm going to starve if I have to use these things," he muttered.

Paolo reached over and adjusted his fingers for him and then after a few more attempts he caught on. The food disappeared quickly. Finally when they could stuff no more in their mouths they stopped. Alicia slid her chair back and let out a very unladylike belch that amazed the boys and elicited a response in Chinese from the distant kitchen. She giggled, covered her mouth, and uttered something back in Chinese.

"I said, 'good food.'" She laughed, and so did the boys.

Doug excused himself to find the rest room. It would have been a perfect evening for Paolo if it hadn't been for that envelope in his pocket. Plans smans. He needed advice. Alicia was his friend and he trusted her. Paolo turned to Alicia and with an urgency in his voice said, "Alicia, I have to talk to you quick, while Doug is gone. Don't ask any questions until I'm done, okay?"

Alicia bent to listen and nodded her head. Paolo told her the story of the man and the envelopes. He told her of meeting Chaplain John and giving the envelope to him. He spoke in a rush and she interrupted only once or twice to clarify a point. When he was done she asked, "You have that envelope with you?"

"Yes."

"Let me see it."

Paolo produced the envelope. It was folded in half and a little crumpled but the writing on its surface was plainly visible. "Give this to Orly Mann."

"Give it to me," Alicia said. Paolo did and to his consternation she disappeared into the kitchen with it.

A gentle answer turns away wrath, but a harsh word stirs up anger.

Proverbs 15:1

"Yeah, I get aggravated about certain things from time to time. I get aggravated when I don't run better. If I didn't I wouldn't need to be here."

Bill Elliott, Winston Cup driver, car #94

WHEN ALICIA GOT up so suddenly and left the room with the envelope, Paolo's stomach lurched. It was not a good feeling considering the large amount of Chinese food that he had just packed away. Two seconds later, Doug was back.

"Where's Alicia?" he asked.

"I'm not certain, probably same place as you. Who knows where girls go?" Paolo replied irritably. *Where is she?* he thought. *And what is she doing with that envelope?*

Doug cleared his throat. "Paolo, can I ask you something? Something real personal?"

"Sure."

"When did you become a Christian? When did you make a choice that putting your faith in Jesus, or whatever you call it, was the right thing to do?"

Paolo snapped suddenly to the real world. All thoughts of Alicia were quickly placed on the back burner. He could tell by the hard look on Doug's face that he was sincere. His hands were on the table, but his fists were tightly clenched and he was staring intently at Paolo with narrowed eyes.

Paolo breathed a quick prayer. *Lord Jesus, give me the right words to say that might comfort my brother. I don't know what is going on in his head, but he obviously is thinking hard about something and it looks like you might be involved. Give me your words to speak.*

"I guess I've been going to church my whole life, Doug. Me and Alicia plus a few other kids in the youth group too. Some of us have known each other since grade school. I guess I always considered myself a Christian, but then two years ago when I was a sophomore the youth group went on a retreat. The speaker was okay but nothing extra special. But I got to tell you, God used him in a special way. He challenged us to spend time in God's Word. You know, the Bible. I was just a kid, but I started reading, and then I began to notice something about myself. I was the most anxious person on the face of the earth and I was scared by everything. I was afraid of the dark. I was afraid to ride the bus. I was afraid of other kids. I was afraid my parents were going to get a divorce. I was afraid of dying. Man, you name it and I was scared of it. Not just the usual scary stuff but just about everything. Anyway, one day I read this verse in Philippians 4:6–7 that says,

Do not be anxious about anything, but in everything, by prayer and petition, with thanksgiving, present your requests to God. And the peace of God, which transcends all understanding, will guard your hearts and your minds in Christ Jesus.

"It had such an impact on me that I memorized it. Well, that was me. Worrying about everything. So I worried about that passage for a while, and I would quote it to myself. I still wasn't certain what it meant. I mean, everybody is anxious and some of us are anxious most of the time.

"Well, then I went in to see Tom. He explained to me all about God's peace and not worrying about stuff, and then he challenged me to lay everything at the feet of Jesus and place my faith in him. Well, I did.

"It doesn't mean I don't get anxious man; oh, man do I! But the truth is I can lay that stuff down before God's throne and do my best to trust him to work things out his way.

"I don't know if that answers your question, but that is what it means to me to trust Christ." The words had poured out of Paolo, and he took a minute to catch his breath.

"Oh yeah, it also means that my sins are forgiven and I can live a life that is pleasing to God. It's okay for me to say no to things God doesn't want me to do, and it is plenty okay for me to say yes to certain stuff like having fun with my friends. One thing that Tom always says is that when we live a life pleasing to God we are living a life that is pleasing to ourselves as well. God doesn't want us to not have fun or anything; he just knows what is best for us."

Doug listened intently as Paolo spoke. Then Paolo said, "Let me ask you a question, Doug. Have you placed your faith in Christ?"

Doug looked down at the tabletop and furrowed his brow. "My dad and mom are Christians . . . and Dad up and left us. I've been to church most of my life, like you, but I never really believed in Jesus. I guess I just never felt the need. I know about some of the people in church—they do things that are as bad as anybody else. In fact, you know what, Paolo? Some of the folks I know that don't go to church are more honest than those that do. I don't know if I'm ready to trust God or anybody else, Paolo. I'm tired of people saying one thing and doing something else."

Just then, Alicia came through the door of the room with a half smile on her face. "Whoa. What happened? Did somebody die? You guys look serious. Come on, let's get out of here and get some air."

Doug reached for his wallet.

"No, no," said Alicia. "If you try to pay, Aunty Grandmother will pinch more than your cheek. She is a very generous person and besides, she loves me." Then she tossed her long hair.

They popped through the door into the street. The fresh night air was invigorating. As they headed back up the hill toward the cable car stop, Alicia dropped back and pulled Paolo with her. She quickly slipped him the envelope which he just as quickly stashed in his pocket. Then she handed him a sheet of paper folded into squares.

"This is a copy of what the envelope has in it," she whispered in Paolo's ear.

Paolo looked at her with wide, accusing eyes. "How did you . . . ?"

Alicia quickly put her finger to her lips and said with a mocking Chinese accent, "Shhh. Ancient Chinese mystery having to do with boiling water, steam, and that modern invention held by Aunty Grandmother called copy machine. Ancient Chinese kitchen have lots of boiling water and ancient Chinese Aunty Grandmother have ancient, but working, copy machine." She rolled her eyes and gave Paolo a wink.

"Did you reseal the envelope?" he asked, while reaching in his pocket and fingering the edge of the envelope.

"Sure did, Pally. Used a little glue. No one will be the wiser. But you know what? There was nothing but one sheet of paper with a list of nine-digit numbers. That's it. No message, nothing else. Just one sheet. I wonder what it means?" she asked.

"Man, Alicia, I don't have any idea what it means. I only know I have to get it to Orly Mann somehow or Doug is in trouble. I wonder—how am I going to do that?" Paolo rolled his eyes and put both his hands in his back pockets in a dejected manner. Alicia snuggled close to him and looped her arm through his.

"God will make a way, Pally. He is faithful. We can trust him," she said.

The cable car was just cresting the hill and with a happy grin on his face, Doug was waving to them to come on.

He looks like he is really having a good time, Paolo thought. *Maybe what I need to do is let him in on what is going on. Maybe he knows something or could add some*

91

light to this thing. But I don't want him to get hurt, he agonized with clenched fists.

Just as they started running up the hill to catch the cable car, Alicia quickly turned to him and said, "Pally, I think you ought to consider telling Doug. He is your only way to get the envelope to Orly Mann, isn't he?"

Oh great, Paolo thought, more puzzled than ever.

In his motor home Bear sat in front of the computer console with red-rimmed eyes. It was late and he was tired. He wasn't getting anyplace at all. He had analyzed every suspension part that had turned a lap on a racetrack and that had been used on one of their race cars in the past few months. He'd been over invoices and checked sources and part numbers. He'd cross-referenced the laps run on the cars that crashed and attempted to find a correlation between wear patterns and suspension settings. Different shock absorbers placed heavier loads on suspension components in different situations. The banking in the corners was different on each of the three different racetracks where they had crashed. Sears Point was the first road course they had run so far this year, and turn ten was flat with no banking at all. It didn't make sense. Corner load put stress on different parts, and when trailing arms and track bars were changed the whole parameter of load stress went south for the winter and daffodils were growing out of his ears.

Unknown to anyone but himself he had salvaged the spindles from the three previous crashes and brought them along. He also had pulled the broken spindle off the car wrecked this morning. All four of the broken pieces were laid out on a red shop rag on the table next to the computer console. As soon as the pits opened tomorrow morning he was going to pull the same part off the car that Orly had used to qualify. It wasn't broken completely yet and maybe its wear pattern could tell him something. Something was bound to match up and give him insight to all of this. It just had to. There was a solution out there somewhere. He wiped his red eyes, dumped the program he was running, blew his nose, and headed for the bunk, muttering to himself.

An hour later he was still muttering as he tossed and turned and computed stress loads in his head.

When Pastor John opened the envelope and saw the money, he quickly put it in his pocket. This wasn't the place to drag a big wad out and count it. Too many people were still walking around. As the pits emptied, he quickly said his farewells and trekked up the hill to his own motor home. He sat down at the table, dumped the money out in front of him, and began to count. The hundreds were fresh and crisp and wanted to stick together. He counted it twice just to make sure. The total was $25,000.00. There was no other note, just the white business card with the words carefully printed that said, "Give this to the Prescotts."

His wife came from the back of the motor home, drying her hair with a towel. She whistled when she saw the pile of money.

"Good grief, John, what did you do, hold up the ticket office?"

"No, I didn't hold up the ticket office. But it might be easier to explain if I did," he replied. Then he told her the story.

Being a pastor's wife she was used to the unusual, but it still seemed a rather odd series of circumstances. Well, God worked in mysterious ways and Maggie Prescott certainly could use the money. Bud's leaving was mysterious in itself. John and Martha probably knew as much about it as anyone else and that wasn't much.

Maggie had told them that she wasn't at liberty to tell all the details—that Bud had some "family" business to take care of. And that was all she'd say. He'd come home from his work in Orly's shop late one Thursday evening, packed a few clothes, went in and kissed the kids in their beds, gave her a hug and a kiss on the cheek, went out the door, climbed in his truck, and she hadn't seen him since. That was a little over three weeks ago. He asked her to call Bear in the morning and tell him he was gone and didn't know when he would be back. But that he *would* be back. It wasn't like Bud to do this. He was a hard-working man and loved his wife and kids. He had a special relationship with Doug, and it seemed strange that he would abandon them all with no explanation. When Bear got the lowdown from Maggie he then called John and asked if he and Martha would stop by.

John and Martha went over to see Maggie, and she told them everything would be fine. No, they weren't fighting. No, there was no reason to expect foul play and no, she didn't want to call the authorities and no, she didn't need any help. She would manage. It was just a "speed bump" in life, she'd said. Maggie was a responsible woman and the Prescotts were very much capable of taking care of themselves. Her only real concern was how Doug would handle not seeing his dad for an extended period of time.

After a long talk, John and Martha said their farewells—they had done what they could and would check in on occasion to see if everything was okay. Maggie promised to keep them posted.

Orly and Bear had decided to keep Doug on the crew and let him travel with them. John saw him on a number of occasions and made a special effort to stay close to Doug at the racetracks. Doug was a likable kid and everybody kind of kept an eye on him. He'd confided to John just the other day that "he was sure tired of answering questions about his dad. Why did they ask him anyway? He didn't know any more than anyone else."

John decided he'd better get on the phone and give Maggie a call to tell her that he had a substantial wad of money to get to her and ask how she wanted him to send it. In all his years of ministry, John had given many people many different messages. Some good and some not so good, but he had never had the opportunity to tell someone that a stranger had given an envelope full of money to another stranger who in turn had given it to him to give to the Prescotts. This ought to be an interesting phone call.

It was late when the boys dropped Alicia off at her place. They waited until she got in the door and then drove back to Paolo's house. His folks were in bed, and the boys quietly headed up the stairs to Paolo's room. His mom had made up the extra bed, and Doug sat down on it and tested the springs.

"Boy, you've got a lot of posters and stuff," he said as he looked around the room. Practically every inch of wall space was covered with posters and promo pictures of drivers and race cars. Some were even autographed.

"Man. Paolo, for a guy who has never been to a race you have a pretty good collection. What did you do? Send away for all of this stuff?"

"Yeah, I joined a few fan clubs and got some stuff. It's my hobby. Sometimes I dream of what it would be like, you know, being on a team and maybe traveling . . . you know, like you do, Doug," Paolo said as he emptied his pockets on the top of his dresser. He was so tired he could hardly keep his eyes open. The envelope came out and he unconsciously put it with the rest of his stuff as he slipped into his pajamas.

"Yeah, I have to admit it is fun to travel with the team, but it can get boring. Everything up to race time is a preliminary, sort of. Then when race time comes on Sunday, things get really serious. Before you know it, the race is over, for good or bad, and you pack up the whole show and head back to the shop to sort out the pieces and get ready for the next weekend." Doug said this as he slipped off his sneakers and lay down on the bed.

"My dad has worked for a lot of different teams. He started taking me with him when I was just a little kid. We've slept in a lot of cheesy motel rooms and eaten a lot of greasy racetrack food. Then when he got to know Orly, and Orly got his own team, things changed. Orly takes very good care of his people, and he has great sponsorship, and he keeps a great shop. It's so clean in there you could eat off the floor—I'm not kidding. Maybe you could come to

Charlotte sometime and see what the shop looks like and I can show you where I live."

Doug continued to rattle on as Paolo collapsed on his bed. In what seemed like only a couple of minutes he was snoring gently. Doug continued to talk with his hands behind his head until he noticed that Paolo was dead asleep and he was talking to himself.

He got up and began to get ready for bed himself. He emptied his own pockets and placed his change and keys in a pile next to Paolo's. He casually noticed the manila envelope and thought nothing of it until he spied Orly's name on it.

Wonder what this is? he thought, as he turned the envelope over. *Maybe it's just something Paolo wants Orly to autograph.* People were always sending stuff to Orly to sign. Ticket stubs from the races he'd won, or programs, stuff like that. Orly did his best to sign them and then send them back. Ah well, he'd ask Paolo in the morning if he wanted him to have Orly sign it. Doug turned the light out and went to bed.

Alicia gulped down a glass of orange juice, wiped her lips on a napkin, gathered her things, and charged out the door, yelling good-bye to her mom as she went. She was a little late, as usual, but she still had enough time to catch the Muni bus to work if she hustled. A few minutes later she was seated and heading up Geary Street to her Saturday job. It was a bit of a drag working on Saturdays, but it paid well. She could make more in six hours punching numbers into a computer than other kids working at

McDonald's all week long. Actually it was easy but it could be pretty boring. She worked for a large Chevrolet dealership and kept track of their parts inventory by punching in part numbers and coordinating invoices and billing sheets. Usually she was done in about six hours, which gave her the rest of the afternoon to goof off. As she rode along she rehashed the events of the previous evening in her mind. Pally's friend Doug was cute and seemed to be a really nice guy. She knew it was pretty exciting for Pally to have someone to talk to about racing. Not too many kids on the West Coast knew much about racing, at least not like they did in the East, and she was glad Pally had a friend who was involved in it. She sure didn't know much about it. She didn't even like cars much.

Tough thing about his dad and all. Sometimes the ways of so-called adults seemed very hard to understand. Probably the way Jesus feels about us, I imagine. Interesting story that Pally told her about Doug and the envelopes. She rummaged in her purse to find her lip gloss and saw the letter she had copied for Paolo. When she made a copy for Pally it was just an extra second's work to make a copy for herself. Pally would be mad if he knew, but she liked a mystery just like anyone else. Besides, if and when Pally found out, he wouldn't stay mad at her for long. He never could. She knew she frustrated him sometimes, but that was okay. He was too tense anyway. He loved her. He didn't know it yet, but he did, and if God was willing maybe someday they would get married. She knew that much in her heart.

She thought about the sheet for a minute without taking it out and looking at it. It had looked pretty boring actually. Wonder what it meant. Maybe it was a code of some sort. Visions of her and Pally in black overcoats and old-fashioned hats filled her mind, and she covered her mouth as she giggled out loud.

After a good Mama Pellegrini breakfast, the boys hit the road. Paolo was tired and frustrated. The Chinese food from the night before hadn't set all that well. He slept in fits and bunches, tossing and turning. He still hadn't made up his mind about what he should do. If he told Doug, Doug's life could be in danger. Maybe he just ought to go to the cops. If he didn't tell Doug, he wasn't sure how he was going to get the envelope to Orly.

All this was working in his mind plus the fact that he just wasn't a morning person. Mornings were for sleeping, and the only thing he had to look forward to was a long day in the Chicken Shack.

Doug, on the other hand, was bright and fresh as if morning was the best part of the day. He was pleasant and very gracious to the Pelligrinis, talking a mile a minute. At least, when he could get a word in with Mama Pellegrini.

The fog had rolled in sometime in the wee morning hours, and as the boys crossed the Golden Gate Bridge it made the morning gray and wet. The old Chevy purred along as they headed north on Highway 101 toward Sears Point.

"Can't see much this morning, can you? That fog is sure pretty thick," said Doug. "I sure want to thank you, Paolo, for having me at your house. Your folks are very nice and it was good going to your church and all. Alicia seems like a real nice girl. She is pretty funny. I'll never forget our time in Chinatown at her Aunty Grandmother's. Must be interesting living in San Francisco." Doug kept up a running commentary as they drove down the freeway. Paolo responded with grunts and noncommittal noises, but Doug didn't seem to notice. Just as they were taking the off-ramp for Highway 37 and Sears Point he said, "Oh, hey, by the way, if you want me to have Orly autograph whatever is in that brown envelope, I would be glad to have him do it for you. In fact, if you want some more racing stuff I can get a lot of things from the other teams. We've got quite a bit ourselves, I think. They give out a lot of free stuff. I know most of them and I'm sure they would pass their promotional junk along. Hey!" At the mention of the envelope Paolo had jumped in his seat and nearly lost control of the car. "Watch out, Paolo. You still sleeping or what?"

Paolo's mind raced for a minute then slipped out of gear as his temper got the best of him. The frustrations of the previous night and the burden of the envelope were just too much.

"No! I've got nothing for Orly Mann to sign. What made you think I did?" Paolo's face was instantly red.

"I saw you had an envelope with Orly's name on it and thought maybe you had something for him. People do that all the time," Doug said in a small defensive voice.

"Gee whiz, Doug, what did you do?" Paolo yelled. "Go through my stuff while I was sleeping last night? I invite you to my house and you go messing around with my stuff. Not cool, man." Paolo's tone was obnoxious and irritable. He knew he would be sorry later.

Doug was immediately offended that his new-found friend would think he would do something so rude as to go through his stuff. He wasn't at all prepared for Paolo's anger. He abruptly closed his mouth and folded his arms in hostile silence. The silence became awkward and tense. Paolo pulled into the vendors' entrance to the racetrack as Doug said, "Just drop me off here. I can walk up the hill. Thanks for the fun time. I'm sorry you don't trust me, Paolo. I would never go through anybody's stuff. I thought you were different, but you are just like all the other Christians I know. You talk a lot about loving other people. But when it comes down to it, it doesn't mean much. See you around some time." With that he was out of the car and walking up the hill.

Paolo pulled into the vendors' parking lot and slammed the old Chevrolet into park. He was immediately aware of what a jerk he had been. The tired shift linkage on the car rebelled at that point and promptly broke into two pieces. Paolo pounded the steering wheel in frustration. He had let his temper get the best of him and said a really stupid thing to a good friend. Now his car was broken. And instead of being a spectator at the racetrack, he had to work in the stupid Chicken Shack all day. Then to top things off he still had that envelope to somehow get to Orly Mann.

For he will deliver the needy who cry out, the afflicted who have no one to help.

Psalm 72:12

"Tommy [crew chief] and all the guys on the CAT team kept adjusting and I kept complaining. They'd adjust and I'd keep complaining. I probably sounded like a cry-baby."

Ward Burton, driver of the Caterpillar sponsored Pontiac

A RACE WEEKEND is a lot like a two hundred-pound bowling ball rolling down a hill that gets steeper as it descends. It starts off slow and leisurely, belying the fact that good old momentum is starting to build. By the time it gets halfway down it is moving pretty good, and as it approaches the bottom it is really flying.

Saturday is halfway down the hill. The fastest twenty-five cars are already in the race. The rest would re-qualify in the afternoon or sit on their time, hoping no one knocks them out of the field. If history serves as the guide, most likely the winner of the race would come out of the top twenty-five. No one had ever come from farther than thirteenth to win. Sears Point was not an easy place to pass and with the new configuration it was even more difficult. It took skill and a great handling car to get around the competition, especially considering that there is only a little over a second separating first and twenty-fifth. The whole field was pretty evenly matched.

Bear knew all this better than most, and he was grumpy. In fact he was as grumpy as an . . . well, an old bear. An old bear that hadn't had much sleep and whose stomach was upset from too much coffee and lead-sinker donuts piled on top of worry. He was making phone calls at daylight on his cellular phone. First he called Orly in his motor home and had a lengthy discussion about certain qualities of various metals. Orly hadn't slept particularly well either, but his insight was good. Then Bear called the engineer-owner of the fabrication shop—in fact rolling him out of bed. He agreed to come down early and open up. As soon as the garage area opened Bear was through the gate and into the pits with single-minded purpose and a zipped-up athletic bag in his hand. The other members of the crew took one look at him and gave each other looks that said, "Be careful!" Bear didn't get like this often, but when something was troubling him and he had that focused no-nonsense look on his face, it was best to speak when spoken to and do exactly what he said without even the trace of an argument or comment.

"Come on, guys, get me that car out of the hauler. We got a lot of work to do if we're going to get this thing to run. Come on, guys, get a move on. Let's go." He shouted and waved his arms for emphasis.

Everybody knew that the car would run. But what Bear meant was *run,* like faster than anybody else's car. The crew hopped to it and soon had the orange and yellow race car parked and up on jackstands. Bear gave a series of rapidly spoken instructions about what he wanted done, then abruptly turned his back and grabbed a handful of wrenches from the immense rollaway toolbox. He waited impatiently as the tire man quickly removed the right front wheel. As soon as he was done Bear pulled his little stool in front of the suspension, sat down, and went to work. Nobody said a word, but every crewman managed to steal a glance or two and knew immediately what he was doing. Twenty minutes later the suspension components, hub, caliper, and brake rotor were laying in a carefully ordered row on shop rags beside the car. Bear's skillful hands knew exactly how to disassemble each component and it wasn't long before he had the spindle and kingpin assembly in his hand. He looked at it like a trophy bass, wiped it clean, and wrapped it in a clean rag. Wiping his hands, he picked up the athletic bag in one hand and the suspension in the other. To no one in particular he said, "I'll be back in a little while," then marched out the pit gate with short, choppy, determined steps.

Bear went to the back of one of the steel buildings that sat on the Sears Point property behind the garage area and into the machine shop that did specialty fabrication for race cars and other high-tech applications.

Now the shop owner and Bear had their heads together over the offending parts laying on the workbench before them. They examined every spindle that had failed. The parts lay there like a plate of pork chops and as they poked and prodded, they looked very much like two chefs discussing the merits of white bread and chestnuts versus cornbread and oyster stuffing.

John and Martha were up early as well. John decided to use one of the pay phones scattered around the track to call Maggie Prescott rather than run the bill up on his cellular. He and Martha enjoyed the fresh coolness of the very early morning as they made the short walk to the public phone. Sears Point sat nestled in a little valley surrounded by rolling hills that were now golden with brown grass. It was hard to believe that tomorrow there would be over one hundred thousand race fans spread out all around the place. But at this time of the day on a Saturday morning, things were still relatively quiet and it was a rural paradise. The grass on the hills was moving in a gentle breeze, and they could hear the meadowlarks and red-winged blackbirds staking out their territory. In an hour the racetrack would start coming alive and there would be hundreds of people at this same spot, but right now it was quiet and peaceful.

It was three hours later on the East Coast, so Maggie had been up for a while. She answered the phone on the second ring.

"Hello," she said. John could immediately hear the tightness in her voice.

"Good morning, Maggie, this is Chaplain John calling from sunny California, and before you ask, Doug is just fine."

"Oh, good morning. Thanks. I was wondering about Doug. You say he is okay?"

"Oh yes, Maggie, he seems fine. Still missing Bud, of course, but he is okay."

Maggie went on, "I was expecting your call. . . . I mean . . . well how are you?"

John had worked with people most of his life and for some reason he felt as if there was a lot more going on here than met the eye, or the ear, in this case.

"Oh, we are just fine. Listen, Maggie, something unusual, but good, has just happened and I wanted to see what you wanted me to do about it." John explained the circumstances and the amount of money that he had been given for them. She didn't interrupt him or make any comment at all. He found that odd.

"You still there, Maggie? I know it sounds a little preposterous, but that is the way it unfolded. What should I do with the money? I could wire it to you or put it in a bank, I suppose. Might be better to get a cashier's check, or I could simply have the bank transfer it to your account. It is a lot of cash and I would like to do something with it pretty soon. Like today."

There was a lengthy pause and John was about to speak again when Maggie said, "Yes, you are right, John. It is a lot of money and it is a bit overwhelming. But I am going to ask you to do a favor for us. Would you just hang on to it until later? In fact, could you bring it back home with you and give it to us then? Thank you, John. You are going to have to excuse me. I have to go now. Thank you for calling." With that she hung up, leaving a very perplexed Chaplain John looking at the dead telephone receiver as if it had bitten him.

"Well, what did she say?" asked Martha.

"She told us to just hang on to it and give it to her when we get home. Didn't even give me a chance to tell her that we are taking the long way to see the kids and won't be back for three weeks. Well, I'm lost. Now what do we do?" he asked as he looked into his wife's face.

"I guess we hang on to it. Could always put it under the mattress, I suppose," Martha said with a furrowed brow. "I know. I'll put it in an ice tray and we can hide it in the freezer."

"How did she seem to you?" Martha asked again.

"Well, you know what? I think she knew about it beforehand. I also think that there is a lot more to this than we know. We will just have to wait to see what happens," John replied, at the same time trying to remember if they locked the motor home when they left. Twenty-five thousand dollars was a lot of money to leave lying around.

"Come on, it is a beautiful morning. Let's go for a walk and enjoy the birds and the country before this place starts going nuts." Martha took his hand as they walked. "Did you lock the motor home?" she asked.

Bear came back a half an hour before the morning practice session and glanced at the car. No one on the crew met his gaze, but everything had been changed on the car per his instructions. It had even been carefully wiped down, and now it gleamed in the morning sun. The right front suspension was all that remained to be finished and it still lay in pieces exactly where Bear had left it. He was whistling as he pulled his little stool over and proceeded

107

to put things back together. Orly came in the gate a couple of minutes later and meandered over to the hauler. He stopped every few feet to sign an autograph for the constant stream of people who followed him. Once he even paused to have his picture taken with a fan and his wife. Finally reaching the sanctuary of the hauler where the car rested, he stopped and looked over Bear's shoulder.

"I knew you'd figure it out sooner or later," said Orly.

"Well, I haven't got it completely figured out, but I think I am on the right track." Bear looked up at Orly. "How you feeling?"

"I'm sore but nothing is broken so I'll be okay. What do you want to do this morning?"

"Why don't you take it out and shake it down some. We can scuff some tires in and bed the brakes a little. Then after we're satisfied with it, you can cut a couple of hot laps and we'll go from there. I want to run a check on the mileage too. I want to make sure that new carb is jetted right. I don't think we or anybody else can do this race on two stops but I want to make certain. Course a lot depends on yellow flags and whatnot. How's that sound?"

"Sounds good to me, Bear. Two stops, huh. I wonder?"

"You know, Orly, you've got your work cut out trying to come through the pack starting twenty-fourth. The crew's been practicing some, and I think we are one of the fastest for tire changes, so we might be able to save you some time in the pits. I do wish we had Bud with us, but we don't and that's that I guess." Bear paused a minute and said, "Passing is going to be real tough. We are just going to have to be patient. But 112 laps is a lot, and if you can keep out of trouble we might do okay."

Orly was an optimist. In fact if truth be known, he fed on adversity. Some of his best runs had come when he started in the midst of the pack. He was one of those drivers that just never gave up—he took advantage of every opportunity to move up a spot. That was why he had won so many races. "Well, you know as well as I do, Bear, that it all depends on the car. If we can get this thing working like we know it can, then we'll have a decent chance at a good finish." Then he added, "Hey, have you seen Doug around? I was wondering if he had a good time last night."

"I saw him a few minutes ago and he had a scowl on his face. Didn't say much except that he had a good time but that something happened this morning."

"If you see him tell him I'm looking for him. We need to get him up to speed on that thing you and I talked about this morning."

Doug was hiding out in the motor home. He was miserable and he didn't quite understand why. Sometimes his feelings just ran away with him. He would get that ache in his throat, and his stomach would feel funny, then the shameful tears would come.

He was bewildered by Paolo's turning on him. He really liked Paolo and then the guy blasted him like that. He didn't do anything except be a friend; he was just trying to help him out. Then the guy got all tipped over and upset.

Ever since Dad left nothing seemed to make sense anymore. It seemed he couldn't trust anyone. The ache in Doug's throat crawled down to his heart and despite his best efforts, hot tears filled his eyes and he began to weep.

Come on, he told himself. *You are eighteen years old. Get a hold of yourself. You shouldn't be crying like a baby.*

I am sick of "shoulds," he said to himself. Then he buried his face in his arms and sobbed. He missed his dad, pure and simple. He was tired of trying to make sense of the whole thing. It was too overwhelming.

He mumbled in a cracked whisper, "Lord, if you are listening to me please hear my prayer and take care of him. I know I haven't been good and I guess I haven't put my trust in you, but please, please, take care of my dad. Please bring him back to us . . . to me, Lord. You know I need him."

Doug was startled to feel someone's arms around him and he stiffened for a minute, then Orly hugged him to his chest. His strong arms and hands held him solid and he cradled Doug's head. When he pulled back Doug could see a sparkle of tears in the race driver's eyes.

"It's okay, Dougie. Let it out. Don't fight it, son. You been carrying a heavy load for a long time." Orly pulled Doug close again, while Doug's shoulders heaved and he sobbed out loud. Finally his tears subsided. Doug pulled away, blew his nose, and wiped his eyes.

He looked up at Orly with a pleading expression on his face. "Sometimes, Orly, I just can't hold it in. The tears come and I feel so foolish, but I don't know how to stop it. I'm a man and men don't cry."

"You are right, Doug. You are a man. But everybody cries sometimes. You can't stop what you feel. Don't worry about showing it. What you are feeling is called grief and it has a way of coming out whether we want it to or not. You are worried about your daddy, and that is affecting you a lot more than you know. You can pretend everything

110

is okay, and sometimes that works for a while, but grief and pain have a way of finding a crack and leaking out anyway. Best not to analyze it. Just let it go and experience it, and then move on. It helps a whole lot if you have somebody to talk to about it," said Orly as he patted Doug's back. "You'll be okay. It will work out. Now wash your face. We got work to do."

Doug turned back to Orly and gave him a quick hug. He wasn't his dad but he was the next best thing. Orly and Bear were pretty special to him.

"Speaking of moving on, we best get down to the pits. I've got to take the car out for a session, and I want you to check something for me," Orly said.

Together they left the motor home and walked down the hill to the garage area.

Paolo was cutting the fat off a pile of chicken halves with a sharp boning knife. He felt frustrated, angry, and incredibly dumb—not necessarily in that order. How could he be so out of control like that? Doug was his friend. He didn't mean to hurt him. In fact, he was trying to protect him. Doug wasn't supposed to know about the envelope, and in his eagerness to keep him safe he hurt the one person he was trying to protect. What was he going to do now? Man, he really'd blown it and blown it good. He threw the chicken into the pot and reached for another off the endless pile in front of him.

They had been studying the Book of Romans in Sunday school and suddenly, almost as if the words were written out in front of him, he thought of the words of the apostle Paul. Paul had gone through the same struggle. They had talked about it in class. In Romans 7:18–20 Paul had written:

> For I have the desire to do what is good, but I cannot carry it out. For what I do is not the good I want to do; no, the evil I do not want to do—this I keep on doing. Now if I do what I do not want to do, it is no longer I who do it, but it is sin living in me that does it.

It was a passage that they had studied in depth, and now Paolo began to understand what it all meant. Even though he was trying to protect Doug, he was allowing anxiety to rule his heart. That was what that peace was all about that he was trying to tell Doug about last night. He had already committed this thing to the Lord. Several times in fact. Now it was time to rest in it.

Then Paolo remembered something his pastor had said last week in church, something from 1 John. Where was that passage? He wiped his hands on his apron and walked over to Uncle Rollie, who was whacking cabbage up for slaw. Uncle Rollie always carried a little New Testament in his shirt pocket. He told Paolo one time that he used to carry his cigarettes there, but when he put his faith in Jesus he gave up smoking. Now when he reached in his pocket he pulled out something that was good for him instead of something that poisoned him.

"Uncle Rollie, can I see your New Testament for a minute?" asked Paolo.

"Sure, Pally, here you go," Uncle Rollie said as he fished it out of his shirt pocket.

Paolo paged through the well-worn little book until he found the passage he was looking for. He read,

> But if we walk in the light, as he is in the light, we have fellowship with one another, and the blood of Jesus, his Son, purifies us from all sin.
>
> 1 John 1:7

Now things were making sense to him. In the process of trying to protect Doug, Paolo had sinned and hurt Doug by falsely accusing him. Paolo couldn't just sit back and trust God to work that out. He had to get to Doug and ask his forgiveness. Their fellowship—their friendship—had been broken and it was Paolo's fault.

He read a little farther;

> If we claim to be without sin, we deceive ourselves and the truth is not in us. If we confess our sins, he is faithful and just and will forgive us our sins and purify us from all unrighteousness.
>
> verses 8–9

Time to get it on and make this thing right. He paused and said a quick, contrite prayer asking God to forgive his sins of anger and his lack of trust. Now he had to get to Doug and ask his forgiveness.

"Uncle Rollie, I'll be back in a minute," he hollered as he took off his apron. "I've got to fix something if I can."

Orly's car was back together and sat waiting to hit the track once again. Bear was satisfied for the moment that things were going to be better. With the race setup installed they would, hopefully, only have to make some minor adjustments. Of course, it all depended on the thing staying together and nobody running into Orly or Orly running into anybody or anything. Any number of a kizillion things could happen when a bunch of drivers whose main job was to stress a piece of machinery to the ultimate limit without breaking it were put together. There was a fine line there somewhere, and finding that line was what separated the "good" from the "there ain't nobody like 'em" guys. In Bear's mind there certainly was nobody better than Orly. *That's what makes racing fun,* thought Bear as he stretched his tired muscles. *It's always a constant challenge.*

Doug was gathering his watches, radio, and clipboard out of the hauler when one of the crewmen yelled to him.

"Hey, Doug, your friend from yesterday is over at the fence. Says he needs to talk to you."

"Yeah, well, I'm not interested in talking to him," snapped Doug.

The crewman shrugged his shoulders and went to his work when Doug stepped around the end of the hauler and saw Paolo outside the chain-link fence that separated the garage area from the public. Paolo was waving his arms frantically and was mouthing words. About that time a race car rumbled by so Doug couldn't hear what Paolo was yelling. He simply turned his back and kept on with what he was doing. He was emotionally drained, and he still had a job to do. He didn't have time for all of this, and what did it matter anyway? He would be on the plane back home to

North Carolina tomorrow night and Sears Point would be just a bad memory. Why bother? He could just wave Paolo off and forget the whole thing.

Despite his resolve, he found himself walking over to the fence.

Paolo was hanging onto the fence with both hands like a prisoner holding onto the bars of a jail cell.

"Doug, I'm sorry. I was stupid. I was tired and I said stupid stuff. I didn't mean to say what I said. I was a toad and totally dumb. I need to talk to you because something is going on. It was on my mind and I said the wrong thing. Look, Doug, you've got to forgive me. You are my friend and I need you," the words poured out of Paolo in a rush.

"You need me, huh?" asked Doug. "What for? So I can get you in the pits and get you some more racing stuff? Is that why you need me?"

Paolo's hands clenched the fence even tighter. "It's not like that, Doug. I was wrong. You are my friend, and you would be my friend no matter if you were on Orly Mann's racing team or not. I told you before, racing is a hobby for me. It isn't the most important thing in the world, and you would still be my friend no matter where or how we met. Please, Doug, I've got to talk to you."

Doug heard Orly's car start up behind him. "Okay, Paolo, I'll talk with you but it will have to be later. I've got to get to work myself. I'll meet you at the Chicken Shack after a while." With that Doug turned on his heel and walked quickly back to the hauler.

A few minutes later Doug was on top of the hauler, listening intently to the radio as Orly shook the car down and warmed things up. Two laps later Orly was making the turn into the pits and came rumbling down the pit lane. He brought the car to a gentle stop and Bear and the crew swarmed over it carefully checking for leaks or anything out of the ordinary.

"Looks good, Orly," Bear said into the radio.

"Okay, Bear, I'm going to take it back out and wring it out pretty good for five laps. Then we'll see what we got." With that Orly was down the pit lane and back on the track.

"Jimmy, you there?" asked Orly into the radio.

Jimmy shifted his ever-present coffee cup to his other hand and keyed the radio. "Yup, I'm here, Orly."

"Everybody, listen up. I'm going to do a little experiment so hold the radio traffic for the next few laps. You ready, Doug?"

Doug keyed his radio. "Yeah, I'm ready, Orly."

Orly put the pedal down and went to work. He tried to be as precise as he possibly could. As he pushed the car into a hard right-hander he coordinated his left thumb with his foot on the brake. When he keyed the mike button the whole crew could hear the noise from inside the car. Then when he lifted his foot from the brake pedal he also lifted his thumb from the mike button. Next time he hit the brakes, down went the button again. Every time he moved his thumb the radio clicked in everyone's ear. Doug was in deep concentration with a stopwatch in front of him. He wasn't watching the track; instead he was timing the duration of the radio clicks and recording them on a sheet of paper. Occasionally he would look up, and when Orly completed a full lap he would quickly flip the sheet over and start another sheet.

After five laps Orly broke the silence and asked, "You got it, Doug?"

"Think so, Orly."

Bear was sitting on the pit wall with his arms folded, watching and listening at the same time. He gave a satisfied nod and climbed down.

"Bring it in, Orly. Let's look at it," Bear said.

Orly idled the car back to the garage area and parked behind the hauler. A few minutes later, Bear had the suspension apart and lying in pieces on the ground. The whole crew including Orly was watching carefully as Bear disassembled the pieces, using gloves so he wouldn't get burned on the still-warm parts.

Alicia was punching computer keys with one hand and eating a candy bar with the other. It was an average Saturday and she had done her job of moving items from invoices to stock programs with her usual quick efficiency. It had been a busy week for the dealership and business had been good. As a result it was later in the afternoon than usual and Alicia still had some work to do. *No big thing,* she thought, *I get paid by the hour, so it's okay. Nothing happening tonight anyway, with Paolo out at the racetrack.*

The candy bar had started to melt so she popped the rest into her mouth and stopped work to look for a Kleenex to wipe her sticky fingers. She rummaged in her purse with her clean hand and couldn't find anything except a folded copy of the letter to Orly. She grabbed it, shook it out, and proceeded to wipe her fingers with it. She glanced back at her computer screen and then glanced back to what she was doing. Suddenly she froze. "No, it can't be," she said out loud.

Two minutes later she was back from the rest room with clean hands and the sponged-off copy of Orly's letter. She carefully smoothed it out in front of her and read it several times with unbelieving eyes. "No! No! No! I can't believe this," she moaned. "I have got to get this to Paolo."

A minute later she had the phone cradled to her ear.

"Hi, Mrs. Pellegrini. This is Alicia. Do you know how I could get a hold of Paolo . . . Yeah, I know there is no phone in the Chicken Shack. Do you think Uncle Rollie might have a cell phone? . . . He does. Great. Do you know the number? . . . You don't. Do you think it would be listed under his name or his business name? . . . You don't know. Is there anyone else I could call that might get a message to Paolo . . . You can't think of anyone. . . . Oh, my mother is fine. Thanks a lot Mrs. Pellegrini."

Alicia hung up the phone in frustration. Maybe she should call the racetrack.

After several fruitless phone calls she went back to work with a vengeance. Her fingers fairly flew over the keyboard, and it was nearly 5:00 when she found herself standing in front of the printer tray waiting for her documents to finish printing. She quickly collated everything and filed them in the proper box. Once again she took the letter out and looked at it.

I don't believe this. How could I be so stupid? She stomped her foot in anger.

If anyone has material possessions and sees his brother in need but has no pity on him, how can the love of God be in him?

1 John 3:17

"We've got a good bunch of people. We're all working hard, and we just want to go a little bit better. We're gonna go home and do our homework."

Mike McLaughlin, Busch Series driver

BEAR WAS SATISFIED. It looked as though they had the problem licked. He had spent the morning at the machine shop with the engineer, pounding their collective experience with metal alloys. They'd run a spectrolysis on the spindle fresh off the car, as well as the other spindles that broke previously in an attempt to find heat changes in the metal. It all had to do with heat—when the brake pedal was pushed it forced the brake pads to make

119

contact with the rotor, which in turned slowed the car. Push the pedal, it forced fluid through the brake line to get a reaction in the caliper. The fluid forced the cylinders in the caliper to expand and press the brake pads against the rotor. The pads worked by friction and friction generated heat. The constant working of the brakes in slowing a 3,400-pound stock car generated a lot of heat. Even with the best of materials the rotors would be glowing cherry red halfway through a race.

The previous suspension failures had taken place at racetracks where brakes were premium. The problem, as Bear saw it, was simple. The heat wasn't dissipating like it should. By changing the location of the brake caliper by a half inch and moving around the ducting that brought cool air to the rotors, they felt they had solved the problem. Orly had worked the brakes hard during this practice session and these spindles looked good. There weren't even any heat check marks on them anywhere. And the color of the metal looked right to Bear's trained eye. The wheel bearings looked fine as well, but he replaced them anyway, making sure to use fresh grease. They were on a roll so they might as well not take chances.

Now that the problem seemed fixed they could really focus on the race setup and get after the serious business of making an honest challenge for the big money. Maybe they didn't have a first place car, but with the right circumstances they had a good chance to finish in the top five. A top five finish would give them a whole bucketful of points and maybe, just maybe, they could start moving up in the standings.

Now there was only one practice session left before the race tomorrow and it lasted exactly one hour. It was everyone's last chance to finalize the race setup on their cars. Everybody called it Happy Hour because it was the last event of the day. Tomorrow the cars would go through the tech line and be pushed out onto the grid. The next time they would be up to speed would be when the race started and the green flag fell. It all better work right then or it would be a long ride home.

Happy Hour is for those that are running okay and smiling but not so happy for those who aren't, Bear thought. He'd been on both sides, and he preferred smiling.

For Paolo the day was dragging on and on and on. It was after 3:00 and the lunch rush had come and gone, and he had seen enough chicken for a lifetime. Today was a lot busier than yesterday as the racetrack began to fill up with the weekend crowd. Paolo had seen the schedule and knew that the last practice—Happy Hour—was at four. If Doug didn't show up pretty soon he wouldn't be here until after the practice . . . or maybe he wouldn't come at all.

Two minutes later he glanced out the window and was delighted to see Doug standing off to the left of the ever-present line of customers waiting for service. He was easy to see in his orange and yellow Orly Mann team uniform but the look on his face wasn't happy. Paolo threw his apron off and ran out the back door. "Back in a minute," he yelled over his shoulder. He flew around the building and waved at Doug and motioned frantically for him to come around.

121

In a minute, Doug came sauntering around the corner with both hands in his pockets and his orange and yellow Orly Mann baseball cap with purple lettering pulled low over his eyes.

Paolo couldn't wait. He started right off, "Hey, man, I am glad you came. I want to say again how sorry I am. I got mad and my temper got the best of me. My mouth overloaded my heart, or as they say in the racing business, my frontside overloaded my backside, and I am sorry." The words rushed out of Paolo with a sort of desperation.

The joke was lame but Doug sort of smiled. "I don't blame you for being mad at me, Doug. I was stupid." Paolo stuck out his hand.

Doug looked him in the eye, pulled his right hand from his pants pocket, and briefly shook Paolo's hand.

Paolo blew out a big puff of air and said, "Pull up a crate, Doug, I got to tell you what's been going on."

Paolo took Doug back to the first time he saw the stranger and then filled in the story from there. At first Doug was mildly interested, but then as Paolo got to the part about the stranger pushing the envelopes through the fence he was intrigued. When Paolo got to the part about him being in danger, Doug was all ears and leaned forward with both hands on his knees.

"Holy cow, Paolo. He said I might be in danger if I knew?" Doug gulped and looked around. "What kind of danger?"

"Don't know. Yeah, he said, just like this, 'Don't tell Doug, *we don't want him to be hurt,*'" Paolo said, mimicking the man's words.

"You say you gave the one envelope to Chaplain John and Alicia made a copy of what was in the one for Orly?" asked Doug. "Do you have it with you? Let me see it."

Paolo dug in his back pocket and brought out the envelope, which was folded in half but still sealed, although somewhat crumpled and smudged by Paolo's nervous hand. Then he reached in his front pocket and pulled out the folded sheet that Alicia had given him. He handed both to Doug and inwardly breathed a major sigh of relief. It was done now. He had told Doug, and his part in this mystery was over. "I've got to tell you, Doug, passing this thing on sure takes a load off me."

Doug took the paper and opened it up. Then he studied it very carefully. He looked up at Paolo after a couple of minutes.

"It's just a list of numbers," he said.

Paolo smirked, "Yeah, I know. Do they make any sense to you?"

Doug continued to look at the paper. "Nope, they sure don't. Maybe they could be part numbers. They look sort of familiar . . . I don't know. I'm not sure. I probably ought to get this to Orly as quick as I can. Maybe it will make sense to him or Bear or somebody. Good grief, this is weird."

Doug went on, "No wonder you were acting so strange and uptight. I was beginning to think you were some kind of nervous freak the way you were jumpy all the time."

"Doug, I think you ought to go give this thing to Orly right now, in case it's something important. I'll see you later," Paolo said, putting his arm around Doug's shoulders.

"Yeah, you are right. Hey, Paolo, I understand why you were upset, man. I'm sorry too, and I am real glad you're my friend. I guess the only thing is . . . I wish you would have told me sooner, but I understand why you were afraid to. I probably would have done the same thing." Doug patted Paolo on the back as he spoke. "I'm sorry I said those rotten things to you about being a Christian and all. You really are a Christian and I know it hasn't been easy for you. This has been an interesting couple of days, and we haven't even had a race yet. Hey, did I tell you Bear and Orly got the suspension thing figured out? They are both smiling now, which is a big relief. I'll come and see you after Happy Hour—if Orly says it's okay." Doug turned and started to walk off.

"Okay, Doug. Take care. Oh, hey, Doug," Paolo yelled. "Do you know anybody around here that has a welder? I kinda broke the shift linkage in my Chevy this morning, and I'm stuck until I can get it welded."

"Sure, no problem. Meet me at the fence after practice, and like I said, if Orly says it's okay I'll come out and help you pull it off. We can fix it up better than new. Actually, why don't you stay with us in the motor home tonight? It'll give us more time to work on it."

Paolo grinned from ear to ear. "That'd be great! I'll give my mom a call to let her know. Cool!" Then Doug turned and walked back into the pits.

It was with a renewed sense of confidence that the Orly Mann Racing Team prepared for Happy Hour. Everyone, including Bear, had a little more spring in their step as they pushed the brilliant yellow and orange car down the hill to the pit lane. Even the large purple 37 seemed to stand taller. Orly was feeling better as he fastened the chin strap on his helmet. The ache in his ribs didn't seem as bothersome, and he was certain that the wholesale changes they had made to this car were going to make it competitive. There is nothing a race car driver hates more than simply riding around a racetrack pushing a sluggish brick of a car and watching people go by him. Real racing takes place up front, positioning for the lead, or better yet leading the whole field.

A few minutes later the track opened for practice and the pit marshal waved the cars out. Orly was one of the first cars in line and he wasted no time in getting down to business. He warmed things up carefully and then started letting the car out like a jockey with a thoroughbred horse.

A good driver knows you never use a car up completely in practice. Some guys get a little carried away, but practice doesn't pay any money. Practice has one purpose— to get the car ready to race for the real money. It is also smart not to let the competition see exactly what you have in reserve. Race cars handle different as the race progresses. A full load of fuel and fresh tires could alter how the car performs and makes it feel much looser. Once the fuel load burns down and the tires get worn in good, you might be able to pick up a second a lap. The characteristics of the racetrack itself often change drastically as the afternoon progresses and rubber builds up on the corners. Let the tires get too worn or too hot and you might lose a second a lap. Stretch the fuel mileage too far, and you could find yourself parked on the back of the course, out of gas, watching instead of racing. Strategy plays an important part in racing. A team not only races the track but they race the other drivers and the pit crews as well. This is a complicated business, and none of the guys at this level are amateurs. They are wily, crafty veterans who have all been here before and know what it takes to win . . . just like Bear and Orly.

Orly let the car out in short bursts. First he hunkered down and pounded the front part of the racetrack, pushing the car to its limits in the first couple of corners. Then he backed off for the next lap and eased his way through the front part of the course, then dynamiting the back section with no holds barred. Periodically he would find another fast car and tuck in behind him just to see how he was handling and how quick he was going in and coming off the corners. Sometimes he could have passed but didn't. Sometimes he let other cars go around him, just to see how it felt to be passed. Aerodynamics played a big part in racing and when a driver passed someone or was passed, it had a tendency to unbalance the car. If that happened in the wrong place at the wrong time, a driver could be collecting paint samples from the tire barriers.

When Orly passed, he passed carefully and was cautious about putting the car at risk. No bumps, no bruises, no scratches. Save it for the money event.

Jimmy sat perched in his familiar spot at the top of the hill in the spotters' observation grandstand. He had a pair of high-powered binoculars around his neck. Periodically he would check certain cars, keeping a close eye on Orly. His comments into Orly's earpiece were even and helpful as Orly worked the two-mile track. Jimmy was constantly feeding him little tidbits about other drivers and conditions on the racetrack.

"Watch that 7 car now when you come up on him, Orly. He's leaking a little fluid of some sort. Might be water or fuel, but it might be oil, so watch out. There is a big chunk of something, looks like tire rubber laying in turn eleven, so watch your line," Jimmy continued in his laconic Texas drawl.

Orly clicked the radio button in response and said nothing as usual. He was busy working in his "office."

Bear was watching everything at once—a skill that he had acquired through the years. He was very mindful of the other competitors and was periodically clicking off differential times with his watch. He was satisfied—they were in the show. They didn't have the fastest car out there right now but they were quick enough. This was a long race and things would change. He knew that and so did Orly. He also knew that he and Orly were the best when it came to making adjustments on the car as the race progressed. It wasn't unusual for Orly to finish a race with a faster car than he started with. A little spring rubber there or a track bar adjustment could make a powerful lot of difference in how a car handled.

Bear was watching Orly as he approached turn eleven and was once again appreciative of Orly's consummate skill as a driver. He was so precise he looked like a freight train on rails. All he needed was a smokestack. This was about a thirty-mile-an-hour corner and required heavy braking and downshifting. Most guys were fishtailing and sliding all over the place, trying to keep their car off the wall. Orly seemed to be getting through it smoother than anyone else. And smoothness meant speed. Speed meant winning. Orly was getting through the speed traps as fast as the fastest because of his smoothness. The car seemed to be handling perfectly.

Orly downshifted and hit the brakes. As he did so, the car made a sudden, lazy, smoke-filled three-hundred-sixty-degree spin right in front of the pit lane, directly opposite Bear. It was like watching a Canada goose in full spread-eagle flight get hit by a shotgun blast. One minute it's soaring in full beautiful flight; the next it's lying on the ground in a crumpled heap. Orly managed to keep the car off the pit wall and it sat forlornly in the middle of the track with gray tire smoke wisping from under the fenders. The cars behind carefully avoided the crippled beast.

Bear's mouth fell open, then he keyed his radio mike, already knowing the answer to the question he was about to ask. "What happened?"

"Suspension broke," said Orly.

Alicia was frantic. She had tried every avenue that she could think of to get word to Paolo. She finally tracked down Uncle Rollie's cell phone number but he wouldn't answer. She kept getting that dumb recording that said, "Your party is either unavailable or out of the area at this time." And she kept getting a recording at the racetrack about ticket sales and so forth. She thought of calling the police, but what would she say? She wasn't completely sure that her information was vital, but she thought that it might be. She just might have to get to the racetrack herself, but she didn't have a car. In fact, she didn't even drive yet.

She dialed the Pellegrinis' house once again and Mama Pellegrini answered the phone.

"Hi, Mrs. Pellegrini. It's me, Alicia, again. I was wondering if you heard from Paolo and knew when he would be home? . . . Oh, good, you did. Did you tell him I was looking for him? . . . Oh, you forgot." Alicia slapped the desk with her hand.

"What! He's not coming home tonight! I see. Yeah, you don't know how to reach him. . . . No, I guess it isn't important," she lied. "Thanks, bye." She hung up the phone. *Now what?* she thought. *Better get on with it,* she decided, picking up the phone again.

Orly, Bear, and Jimmy were again in the lounge section of the hauler commiserating. The previous confident attitude had evaporated like sweat on a hot griddle.

"I'm thinking we ought to pull the car and head back to the shop and start over, Orly," Bear said with a scowl on his face.

"You know we can't do that, Bear. We have sponsor commitments, and it would cost us a ton of money in endorsements and whatnot. Besides we are here and we are qualified," Orly replied.

About that time Doug stuck his head in the doorway.

"I know you are busy, Orly, but I need to talk to you for a minute. It's pretty important. At least I think it is. Kinda strange too. I've got something here that you ought to see."

It was late, and Paolo and Doug were sprawled underneath Paolo's car with flashlights and assorted tools. The shift linkage was refusing to come undone. They had been beating on it for an hour and both boys were covered with dirt and grease. But in truth, they were having a good time. Finally Paolo got the angle he needed with the wrench in the close quarters around the transmission and gave a big yank while Doug held the light, grease running down his bare arm.

"Here it comes, Doug. That bolt is finally moving. Probably hasn't moved in thirty years." The bolt came out and the shift linkage popped loose in a shower of ancient, caked grease and clods of dirt. The boys shimmied out from under the car, spitting dirt and brushing gunk from their hair. Paolo had the linkage pieces in his greasy hand.

"Broke sure enough," said Paolo. "That will teach me to be more careful. Boy, I'll tell you, Doug, the Lord is sure teaching me about my temper. All it does is get me in trouble."

"Too late to get it welded tonight, Paolo. Come on, we'll go up to the motor home and clean up. Maybe find something to eat."

"So Orly didn't show much reaction when he read the list of numbers," said Paolo, changing the subject.

"Nope, it was odd. He read it and then he studied it again. Then he gave it to Bear. I told him about the envelope that went to Chaplain John and what the guy said about me being hurt. He just smiled then and said he didn't think I had anything to worry about. I asked him if he thought it was alright for me to help you with your car and he said, 'Sure. Don't see any reason not to.' That was that and here I am."

"You know, Doug, I don't think I understand anything anymore," said Paolo.

The boys sat down on the ground with their backs against the side of the old Chevy.

"Hey, Paolo, I wonder if . . . nah, never mind," said Doug.

"Wonder what? Go on. You can say whatever it was you were going to say. I'm your friend, Doug. Go ahead and ask."

Doug thought a long couple of minutes and then said, "I was wondering, Paolo, if you would pray with me. I can't hardly keep it together anymore. It just seems like, well, you know with my dad and all. I really feel like God is doing something in my heart . . . I guess what I'm saying is, I want to trust Jesus . . . or however you say it."

To Paolo it seemed the most normal thing in the world that two greasy, teenage boys would be sitting late in the evening with their backs against an old Chevy sharing the Lord. He nodded his head in the dark.

"You bet I'll pray with you, Doug. Are you telling me that you want to trust Jesus as your Lord and Savior?"

"Yeah, that's what I'm saying, Paolo. I want to trust him for me, and I want to trust him to take care of my dad and mom and sister. That's what I want."

Paolo led Doug in a short prayer asking Jesus to forgive his sins and be Lord of Doug's life. Then he prayed for protection for Doug's dad and his family.

"Do you think God heard us, Paolo?"

"Oh yes, Doug. God heard us."

The boys got to their feet as Doug said, "You know, Paolo, I don't think I feel any different, but then maybe I do. Somehow I know Dad will be okay wherever he is."

"God will work things out. You'll see, Doug. Man, I'm hungry."

"Me too. Let's see if we can find something to eat."

"You sure it's okay for me to bunk in the motor home, Doug? I don't want to be a bother with what's going on with the car and all."

"No sweat. Bear and Orly got their hands full. I guarantee they won't even know you are around. We have a couple of empty bunks so there's plenty of room."

Doug jumped up and down on the kick start of the scooter a few times until finally it started. Paolo climbed on the back, and the boys headed up the hill to the compound. The garage area was dark and deserted.

Two hours later Chaplain John was awakened from a deep dream-filled sleep by a knock on the door of his motor home. He was a pastor with a lot of years experience and a late night summons could only mean one thing—trouble or pain of some kind. He said a sleepy quick prayer and asked the Lord to give him wisdom and guidance in whatever situation this might be. He grabbed his robe as Martha whispered.

"Wonder who this is?"

"Don't know," said John. "Best to find out." He turned on the light and headed toward the front of the motor home. Another light knock came as he unlocked the door and flipped on the outside light.

"Why, hello, Bud Prescott. I thought I might see you pretty soon."

Bud Prescott blinked in the yellow porch light of the motor home. He looked very tired. Perhaps exhausted would be more like it. A bone-weary, long-term sort of exhaustion.

"Come on in, Bud. Let me make some coffee."

Bud said nothing as he climbed the steps into the motor home and eased himself into the dining alcove.

He settled himself in the settee. His shoulders slumped as he relaxed in the seat. John sat opposite him as Martha came out in her robe and took over the coffee-making chores. She smiled a greeting at Bud but said nothing.

John waited patiently while Bud collected his thoughts, then said softly, "Let's pray together, Bud." He reached over and took Bud's gnarled, work-worn hand.

"Our Father, you have brought our brother Bud to us for a purpose tonight. We pray that you might give him the freedom to express what it is that you would have him say. He's in need of healing, Father, and we pray that you might touch him. We trust you, Lord God, and we thank you for your love for us. We pray in our Savior's name. Amen."

Bud raised his head and said, "It's over, John." Then his story poured out in heart-wrenching detail. "He's gone, and I've got to tell you it hasn't been easy. I knew he was sick, but I didn't have any idea where he was until he called me a couple of months ago. I wanted to bring him home but he wouldn't hear of it. He was in a hospice in San Francisco when he died—they took good care of him. I guess I should say 'we' took good care of him." John simply sat and listened; Martha quietly placed the coffee cups on the table and sat down next to her husband.

Bud spoke in measured doses. It was his brother Peter who had died. He had been sick a long time with AIDS. It started when he began to run a low-grade fever with flu-like symptoms. He finally had a blood test and discovered that he was HIV positive. Shortly thereafter the virus got serious and put him down hard. Bud knew that he was ill and had been for quite some time. He didn't know that it was AIDS at first, but when he finally heard he wasn't surprised that it was. Peter called late one night a little over three weeks ago and got Bud at the shop. In a weak but frightened voice he told his brother that he was dying and asked if Bud could come. Bud had no choice but to go, but the thing that made it extremely difficult was that Peter wanted him to tell no one. Their parents had long ago passed on and it was just the two brothers. Bud begged Peter to come to North Carolina but Peter refused. He was not only afraid but he was ashamed as well. He was convinced that folks would not only judge him for his lifestyle but that Bud and his family would come under attack as well. Many people got real strange at the mention of AIDS. Peter's initial plan was to simply die and leave a letter to be mailed to Bud after he was gone. But he got scared and came to the realization that he wanted and needed his brother to be with him.

Bud left with no explanation to the kids, making the cross-country trip as quickly as he could. When he got to San Francisco he found Peter in terrible shape, living by himself in a rundown rooming house. At first Bud wasn't certain where to turn, but with a few phone calls and with the help of some compassionate advocates he managed to get help. He placed Peter in a hospice for people with AIDS. It was a place where doctors and nurses did their best to make patients comfortable in their last days. It was also a place that was incredibly sad—there were so many young people suffering there.

Once Bud had Peter settled, he thought many times about leaving him, but he just couldn't. It wasn't easy watching his brother suffer, slowly getting sicker. Peter wanted Bud with him every waking moment and pleaded with Bud to just stay with him for a while. It wouldn't be long. One day turned into another and in retrospect it hadn't been long, but to Bud it had seemed an eternity. Bud was caught between wanting to tell his children, Doug and Melody, what was going on and wanting to respect Peter's wishes. He did tell Maggie, of course, but he swore her to secrecy. People just didn't understand about AIDS and some were quick to judge and condemn. Peter had known this better than most and Bud was learning.

"By the way, how is Doug?" He missed his son so much. "Do you think he will forgive me, John? I should have called him, but I just couldn't. I was with Peter twenty-four hours a day and one day just piled into the next." Bud put his face in his hands for a minute. Then he honked his nose on a dirty handkerchief and resumed talking.

The time in the hospice had been difficult for Bud. Dying of this awful disease was not an easy process and Peter did not go easily. But mercifully, God in his wisdom and in his timing took him home this afternoon. He had been in a coma for three days, and during that time Bud had not only washed his brother's body and sponged his fevered face, he had also filled his heart and head with Scripture. Bud said, "You know, it's an amazing thing, John. Sometimes in the most awful times it seems that God is the closest to us. The medicines seemed to work better when I read the Scriptures to him."

It had taken most of the Prescotts' savings and then some to carry Peter through those last days. But Bud was okay with that and so was Maggie. It was money well spent. At least he had the opportunity to spend time with his brother. Peter had even laughed on a few occasions as they shared old memories and stories. But it was over now.

"I'm feeling pretty low, John, and I am not sure what I am supposed to say to Doug and Melody. I did what I thought was right—I was really struggling. Peter was a good brother, and you know he had a great driving career ahead of him. Doug idolized him. Orly was ready to put another team together for him a couple of years ago, and I guess Peter just couldn't stand the pressure. He up and disappeared and nobody heard from him until he called me. Pretty sad when you think about it," Bud said with a great sigh of resignation. "I hope the kids can find it in their hearts to forgive me for being gone so long. You know, the hardest part of this whole thing was not being around them. I missed my kids, John. I knew you guys would be out here at Sears Point this weekend. I was praying that God would work it out so I could come and see you. I guess I knew Peter was dying but even when he was in a coma I didn't want to leave him. I was afraid he might wake up and I wouldn't be there for him. God worked it out and took him home, and here I am."

"I know you did your best, Bud. You did a pretty hard thing. The kids will be okay. Melody will be just fine. It might take Doug a little while, but he'll come around. He loves you more than you know. He has the highest respect for you. Probably the best thing you can do is level with him. He will respect you even more if you are plain honest with him," said John.

"Yeah, I think you are right. Thanks, John, for your comfort. Maggie said I should come and see you after . . . Peter . . ." Bud honked his nose again.

"Do you know if he is staying in the motor home with Orly, or is he bunking with Bear and the boys? I'm plumb wore out and maybe I'll go over there and crash. I want to see him pretty bad." Bud stretched and rubbed his red eyes.

"I'm not sure where he is sleeping, Bud. One of those two places for sure," John said. "Before you go we have something for you that might help your financial situation some. We don't know where it came from and are just passing it on like we were asked to."

Martha quietly got up and went to the refrigerator and pulled out an ice tray. She set it in front of Bud and said, "There is twenty-five thousand dollars there for you, but you will have to give it a few minutes to thaw out. I think it is a pure gift from the Lord—your sweet wife prayed it in for you."

And we know that in all things God works for the good of those who love him, who have been called according to his purpose.

Romans 8:28

"I think that's the whole deal: desire and determination."
Larry McReynolds, crew chief for Richard Childress
Racing and driver Mike Skinner, car #31

IT WAS DARK and Alicia was scared. It had been quite a night so far . . . and it wasn't over yet. After repeated tries and total frustration in trying to reach Paolo, she decided that maybe the best thing was to just take the information to him at the racetrack. This was hot stuff and for sure she had messed up big time. That guy Orly Mann and some guy named Bear needed to see it. How could she have been so stupid? She had done her best to wipe the chocolate off the letter and had made two clean copies of everything. She had them carefully stapled in a file folder, trying to look as professional as possible. Maybe that would soften the hearts of the people she knew would be upset with her. But how could she get them to Paolo? She had racked her brain trying to think of options and even made a few more phone calls. Kids with cars were few in their large city youth group, and she couldn't think of anyone else that she might trust. Alphonse had a car, sort of, but he wasn't home either. He had a little foreign green econobox. It didn't go very fast and it looked a lot like an old can of peas with a faded label. At least it ran and it could go forever on a tank of gas.

She finally left her job at the Chevrolet dealership and took the bus home. She couldn't ask her folks to take her out to Sears Point; it would just get too complicated and besides, her dad was away on a business trip. She tried Alphonse again and finally got through to his mom, who told her that Alphonse was working at the all-night quick copy place but it was okay to call him there.

When she got through to him he listened for a while and then said, "Alicia, I haven't the foggiest idea what you are talking about, girl. Do you really need me to drive you out to Sears Point, where I've never been, tonight in the dark? Is this really that important?"

"Yes, Alphonse, it is. I need you to do this," Alicia said desperately.

"Okay. Against my better judgment I will do it, only because you are a friend. I get off at 11:00. Be out in front of your house at 11:10. You got money for the bridge and gas? You do know how to get there, right?"

"Yes, I have money, and yes, I'm sure I know how to get there," she replied. "Thanks, Alphonse. You don't know how much I appreciate this."

Alphonse was true to his word and pulled up in front of her house in his econobox to find her waiting on the curb. Her mom was in bed so she left her a note on the counter just in case she was missed. Her mom would worry but maybe she would understand, Alicia thought. Then she thought again. Of course her mother wouldn't understand, and if she got caught she would be in a heap of trouble. But she had no choice. She had to do this. She had caused the problem and the only thing she could do was fix it . . . if she could. Who knew what was at stake here?

Alphonse had been understanding and patient, even when they missed the Highway 37 turnoff because she misread the map and they had to backtrack through Petaluma. Even though it was midnight, the traffic was terrible when they finally found the track.

Across the highway from the track was a large campground reserved for race fans. It encompassed several acres and was jam-packed. For a fee the fans could bring their trailers or RVs or even pitch a tent in this area. Space was at a premium and people were parked almost on top of each other. It seemed every RV or trailer had a flagpole with several flags flying in the night breeze announcing their favorite driver or race team. Loud music blared from several different sources and hundreds of people wearing T-shirts with stylized pictures of their favorite drivers and teams were milling around socializing, even at this late hour. Things could and did get pretty wild in this area and sheriff's deputies and security people were doing their best to keep things under control.

When Alphonse stopped in front of the parking lot leading into the campground area, Alicia came to a grim realization. She really hadn't thought this through—she was unprepared with a plan to find Paolo. The place was enormous and they were expecting a crowd of over 130,000 people in just a few hours. Traffic even now in the middle of the night was backing up. As she studied the chaos, she realized that she did not have even the faintest idea of where to start looking for Paolo. Panic overtook her. She swallowed hard and got a grip on herself.

"I guess I better go in there and see if somebody will give me an idea of where I might start looking for Paolo," she said, looking at a large group of people around one of the many campfires. The light twinkled off the glasses and cans that they held in their hands and their talk was loud and boisterous.

Alphonse was studying the campground as he spoke. "Uh-uh girl. You are not going in there. No sir. Alicia, that's not cool. Ain't no way you are going in there by yourself. And to be honest, having a good-looking African-American young man like me with you isn't going to help our cause either." He looked around and motioned to the road. "Here, let's ask this California Highway Patrol lady directing traffic. She looks cool."

They parked the car and got out to talk to the cop. She was pleasant, considering the circumstances, and listened as Alicia explained her situation.

"You say he is staying at the track with a friend who is part of a race team?" she asked with her hand on her gunbelt and her head inclined to hear Alicia over the revelry and the traffic in the background.

"Yes, that's what his mom said," Alicia said, then added, "He would be with the Orly Mann Racing Team."

The officer pointed across the road. "This is the race-track proper right here, just over this little hill. Right over there by the main gate is where the garage area would be. Just up the hill from there is where they land the helicopters, and just beyond that is the restricted motor-home compound which is where they would probably be." The police officer pointed to a spot down the road close to the main gate. They could just see the shadow of the hill in the darkness. It seemed to be much quieter and less chaotic on that side of the road. "They have pretty tight security over there. There is a fence around the place, but you could talk to the guards at the gate. I doubt if they would let you in there this time of night, though. Maybe you ought to go home and start fresh in the morning." With that she turned and went back to her job of directing traffic. "Good luck finding him," she tossed back over her shoulder.

Alicia and Alphonse got back in the car.

"What do you want to do?" Alphonse asked.

Alicia sat huddled in the seat with her knees together and her head down. "Alphonse, I have to get this stuff to Paolo. I just think it is vitally important. We have to get in there somehow."

"Okay, I hear you." With that, Alphonse started the car and made a U-turn back toward the main entrance gate of the track. He slowly cruised past the multilane entrance. Two hundred yards farther he saw a narrow utility driveway. It was blocked off with a chain strung between two posts and disappeared up the hill between eucalyptus trees.

"If I followed where she was pointing the motor-home compound has got to be just over this hill somewhere," he said, easing over and turning onto the gravel road.

Alphonse pulled up until the chain was resting against the front of his little car. He muttered to himself, "Yeah, I think there is enough slack." He got out of the car and looked around in the bushes for a minute then came back with a board. He motioned for Alicia to get out of the car.

"When I tell you, stick that board under the chain and hold it up as high as you can. I think there is enough slack for me to drive under it. We have to make certain no one sees us do it, though, so you have to be quick."

He waited until no cars were going by, then gave a quick motion to Alicia. Using all her strength, she got the board under the chain and propped it up. Alphonse quickly drove the little car under it, scraping just a little paint off the roof and breaking his radio antenna. As soon as he was through he killed the lights, popped back out of the car, grabbed the board, and stashed it in the bushes for their escape later.

"It's okay, Alicia, I needed a new antenna anyway," he said sarcastically. Then he looked over at Alicia, now sitting very small in the seat. "Hey. I'm sorry. Come on, hang in there. At least we are this far," he said in a kind tone.

Alphonse eased the car along the utility road with the lights off, the engine at an idle, trying to be as quiet as they could. The only sound was the crunching of the tires on the gravel and the quiet purring of the motor. "I'm glad I got my muffler fixed," he said to Alicia. She said nothing. Finally the road paralleled a large cyclone fence and he stopped underneath some trees. They both got out being careful not to make the dome light go on and not to slam the doors. Alphonse could hear his heart beating in his ears. As they stood next to the fence, they could see several helicopters parked, and beyond the helicopters they could just make out another cyclone fence.

"This must be what she was talking about," said Alphonse, pointing to rows of motor homes. Most were dark but some still had an interior light or two on. "Looks like a motor-home compound, and those babies don't look like the average RVs. Some of those things are big as a bus," said Alphonse.

"Yes, I think this is it," replied Alicia. But she still didn't know where Paolo was. He could be in any one of those motor homes, or maybe this wasn't the right place. She started to panic a little. Maybe if she just stood on top of the car and yelled his name as loud as she could, he might hear her. Yeah, him and every security guy for a mile around.

"Alphonse, let's pray."

"Alicia, what are you talking about?"

"I don't know what to do, and I am afraid. Let's pray. Take my hand."

He did as she requested, and she began, "Lord Jesus, please lead us as you see fit. We don't want to get in trouble, but you know I have to do this thing. Amen."

"You can stay here if you want to, Alphonse. I'll be okay now."

"No way, Alicia. I'm here with you. Besides it's dark and I'm afraid of the dark. Let's go stash the car under the trees."

They quietly pushed the little car so it was nearly covered by the brush under the trees. Then they worked their way back to the fence.

"Think you can climb this fence with me?" Alphonse asked in a whisper.

"Give me a break, Alphonse. I didn't take gymnastics for five years for nothing." Alicia buttoned the file folder inside her jacket and bent over to tighten her sneakers. Then she jumped up and grabbed the mesh, lithely scaling the eight-foot fence with an economy of motion. At the top, she flipped her leg over and came down the other side hand over hand. In just a few seconds she lightly dropped to the ground. Alphonse was not as agile and a lot heavier, but he managed to get over. He dropped down beside her out of breath.

"Now what?" he gasped.

"Now we find Paolo," said Alicia in a determined voice.

It was late, past one o'clock, and Orly and Bear were on their second pot of coffee in Orly's motor home. Orly had the letter spread out on the table between them as they studied the numbers once again.

"Well, Orly, we know what these numbers are, but we still don't know what they mean," Bear said as he dunked half a stale donut in his coffee.

"I wish Wiley would have talked to us instead of just giving the envelope to the kid. He must not have been able to get ahold of us or something. I thought I gave him the private cell phone number, but I guess we were busy all day. The only thing I can figure is that he thought he gave us what we needed and we would understand. Doesn't make sense to me. We can't get hold of him now because he's on his way to Japan for that engineering convention. I wish I knew where to reach him. Sure seems strange," Orly mused.

Wiley was a manufacturing representative for an engineering company for the racing business. After an eighteen-hour flight he was sitting in his hotel room eating a Japanese room service equivalent of breakfast, or was it lunch, maybe dinner. *With the time change who knows,* he thought as he moved what he hoped were scrambled eggs around his plate.

Orly had asked him to do a little research on the front suspension components of the race cars, especially the wheel bearings to see if he could help them figure out why things were breaking. Wiley was a savvy engineer. He and Orly and Bear had worked closely together on many different projects. He'd done the research for them and sure enough had come up with a solution for the problem. It was simple really and no problem to fix. Wouldn't take much at all. It boiled down to the right combination of parts and lubrication. A little correction and they would be right as rain.

He had given the envelopes to the boy he'd seen with Doug. He would have come in the pits and given the one envelope to Orly or Bear himself but for the simple reason he didn't have a pass and was already late getting to the airport. Sometimes getting a pass could take thirty minutes or longer. He had seen Paolo behind the Chicken Shack while he was trying to find someone he knew who could give the information to Orly and that other envelope to Chaplain John. A few minutes later he saw Doug and Paolo together and Paolo seemed like a good choice to pass on the envelopes.

He had no idea what was in the envelope for Chaplain John and was simply passing it on as a quiet favor for a friend with the accompanying message about not wanting Doug to know so he wouldn't be hurt by it. He knew it probably had something to do with Bud and his disappearance but it wasn't any of his business. Sure was thick and heavy though. At any rate it wasn't his concern. He said he would do it and he did. No questions asked.

He knew that when Orly read the material in the envelope, it would be self-explanatory. No need to contact the team. They would know what to do. As he finished his breakfast, which wasn't half bad, he laid back on the bed and put the envelope thing out of his mind. It was taken care of. He fully expected to read in the sports section of tomorrow's paper that Orly had a decent finish at Sears Point. He was one of the best drivers Wiley had ever seen, and he had seen a few in his lifetime. With Bear as a crew chief they were tough to beat.

"Well, Orly, I'm going to bed," said Bear as he got up and brushed donut crumbs off his shirt. "We will just put it together with fresh parts tomorrow and hope the thing stays together. Dog, I hate this," Bear said vehemently. "It ain't right, Orly, this ain't right and I don't like it."

"Yeah, I know, Bear. See you in the morning." Orly yawned.

Bear opened the door of the motor home and started to step out.

"Hey! For crying out loud, you scared me!" yelled Bear as he stepped back into the motor home. He looked down into the startled faces of two teenagers. He said back over his shoulder to Orly, "Couple of kids out here, nearly made me jump out of my skin. What are you kids doing here? This is a restricted area—you're not supposed to be here. Besides it is one in the morning. Maybe I better call security."

The girl put her hand on her heart and blinked her eyes before she spoke, "Excuse me, could you tell me where I might find Paolo Pellegrini?"

Orly came up behind Bear and looked over his shoulder. "Paolo, oh, you mean Doug's friend?"

"Yes, that's him," she said, her face brightening and then she looked at Bear's uniform, which had written across the chest, Orly Mann Racing. She looked again at Bear and asked, "Are you Orly Mann?"

"No, I ain't, but he is," Bear said, motioning over his shoulder at Orly. "It is a little late for an autograph."

"My name is Alicia Chen and this is my friend Alphonse. Mr. Mann, I need to talk to you," said Alicia, ignoring Bear. "I have done something very terrible. Could we come in please?"

Alicia settled herself behind the table, said a silent prayer, unzipped her jacket, took out the file folder, and began to talk in a soft voice with measured rehearsed tones. She had been thinking about this moment all day.

She had hoped to talk to Paolo first, but she knew she ultimately would have to apologize to Orly Mann. Here she was face-to-face with him. It was a bit overwhelming, but she plowed on.

Orly and Bear listened intently as she filled in the details of the night with Doug and Paolo. While she talked, she nervously put the folder on the table and smoothed it with her hands.

"When I took the letter from Paolo, I opened the envelope and made a copy for Paolo and one for me and then put what I thought was the original back in the envelope. It wasn't until this afternoon that I discovered that I had made a terrible mistake, two mistakes actually. I didn't put the original back in the envelope; I put a copy instead, and I also forgot to look on the back of the original, which was really the front and has a whole lot of information on it. My Aunty . . . uh has a very old copy machine and I didn't see what was on the back, which was, like I said the front. What I mean is that you only got part of the information that was in the envelope." Despite her best efforts Alicia started to cry.

Bear and Orly exchanged looks. "Is this it?" Bear asked, reaching for the file folder.

"Yes," said Alicia, great tears running down her cheeks as she handed it to him. "I am very sorry and very ashamed." Alphonse, seated beside her, patted her shoulder in sympathy.

Bear flipped open the folder and started to read, "Yeah, here is the note from Wiley. Even signed it. He gives us a detailed description of the problem. Says the numbers on the back, which is all we had, are part numbers of wheel bearings that we should look out for. We knew they were part numbers and we knew they were wheel bearing numbers.

"Well, I'll be. It's the grease, Orly. It's a combination of the grease and the bearings. This says that certain alloys used in the wheel bearings react with certain compounds in certain types of lithium grease. The alloy still rolls freely, acting like a bearing should, but with that type of grease it generates terrific heat. The heat scores the spindle, and then the alloy in the spindle crystallizes and gets super hard and fractures. Then it is only a matter of time till the spindle breaks and Orly Mann winds up on his head." Bear looked up with an amazed smile on his face. "See, Orly, we were on the right track. I told you it was heat and that something was going on there. That is what Harley said this morning when I took those spindles over to his shop. I just knew it." Bear was up and marching back and forth in the limited aisle space of the motor home, waving the letter around like a banner. We couldn't get a handle on it because sometimes I used a different grease when we packed the bearings and sometimes when I used the wrong grease we used a bearing with a different alloy. That is why we couldn't track the variables.

"Little girl, you done just fine to get us this information and we appreciate it. This is something we can fix and we can fix it easy." His eyes were dancing as he patted Alicia on the hand.

"Folks make mistakes, girl. Happens all the time. Don't fret about it. You did what you needed to and got us the information. We appreciate it. Thank you. Wasn't your fault really. Wiley should have made the effort to put it into our hands." Then he said to Orly, "I've got to go. I got to get some sleep so we can be in the garage the minute it opens. I'll see you then." With that Bear was out the door still waving the folder around like a prize and practically skipping across the dirt to his own motor home.

Alicia sat with her head bowed and tears running down her cheeks. Orly reached across the table and patted her folded hands.

"I am very sorry, Mr. Mann. I did a very stupid thing. Please forgive me," she said with tear-filled eyes.

"Of course I forgive you, Alicia. You made a mistake, that's all. No problem. It will be just fine. We really appreciate you coming here tonight, like Bear said. I imagine it wasn't easy for you to get here. How did you get into the compound anyway?"

Bud felt drained and filled at the same time as he left the Mobile Chapel. He had done a difficult job that had taken every ounce of his strength in taking care of Peter. Peter was gone now. It would take him a while to realize that, but it was over. On the other hand, he was filled with a sense of peace that could come only from the Lord. He had done what he felt God had called him to do and there was comfort and security in that. *God always promises to supply the strength for any job he asks us to do,* Bud thought. The job was done.

Now more than anything he wanted to see his family, and Doug was sleeping right here. Silently he opened the door to the motor home and eased inside. He knew the layout and in fact slept here many times himself at various racetracks.

The twenty-five thousand dollars was an incredible gift. He thought he might know where it came from, but it was given anonymously and he would ask no questions. It came from the Lord, and it would certainly help offset a great deal of the cost in taking care of Peter. His medicines and care had been expensive. Bud breathed another quick prayer of thanks. That money had represented the Prescott family savings. Maggie reassured him that God would respect their willingness to help Peter. He sure had. God had just replenished their storehouse. Pretty amazing.

There was Doug, peacefully sleeping with one arm thrown over his head like he had done most of his life. Bud flashed back to when Doug was a little blond-haired boy who used to follow him around the house. No matter what Bud was doing, Doug felt like he needed to be involved. What a joy he had been as a child and now he was a young man. *He has grown up while I wasn't looking or taking notice,* thought Bud. He knelt beside the bunk and smoothed Doug's hair off his forehead. Doug opened his eyes and looked into his face. "Hey, Dad," he said.

"Hello, son. How are you?"

You need to persevere so that when you have done the will of God, you will receive what he has promised.

Hebrews 10:36

"So many times, you don't know what's going to happen.... You gotta stay on your toes and just make the right moves."

Terry Labonte after winning the closest Busch race ever
(2/1,000ths of a second)

THE ALARM WENT off and Bear's eyes flew open. He was out of bed in a flash and was already shaving before he happened to glance in the mirror and see over his shoulder that somebody was in the empty bunk. It wasn't Paolo because he was in the back with Doug. He looked a little closer and realized that it was Bud Prescott. Bud groaned and stretched his arms outside the covers.

"Good morning, Bear. How are you this fine bright morning?"

"Good morning yourself, Bud Prescott. You here for real, or am I just seeing things in my early morning state?"

"Nope, it's me Bear. I'm here and I'm real," said Bud.

"Well, I'm glad. You ready to go to work? I'm thinking we are going to need somebody quick to change that right front tire today. The crew is tired of me bumbling around."

"If you'll have me and I ain't fired, I would be proud to help out some."

"Done. I think there's a uniform for you in the back closet. I brought some of yours from the shop just in case. Now we better get a move on 'cause we got some work to do before the race.

"Hey, you boys back there, let's get going. We've got to bear down this morning. We've got lots to do," yelled Bear.

Paolo's eyes flew open and so did Doug's. Doug didn't say a word as he jumped out of his bunk and raced down the short hall of the motor home.

Paolo rolled over on one elbow to see where Doug was going in such a hurry when he heard him exclaim, "Dad, it *is* you! I wasn't dreaming after all! You are here! Hey, Bear, it's my dad. Hey, Paolo, it's my dad. He's here! I knew you'd be here," he shouted. "I knew it wasn't a dream. Hey, Paolo, God answered my prayer."

Paolo got out of bed and looked down the hall to see Doug hugging a tall man while the man lifted him off the ground.

Doug turned and looked at Paolo. "Paolo, this is my dad, Bud Prescott. Dad, this is my good friend Paolo Pellegrini."

Paolo stuck out his hand. "Pleased to meet you. I've heard a lot about you."

The smell of coffee woke Alicia from a deep dreamless sleep. She rolled over in her bunk and tried to remember where she was. Oh yeah, she was in Chaplain John and Martha's motor home. She and Alphonse had talked with Orly for a few minutes and everyone agreed that it was too late to head back to the city that night. Orly lived by himself in his motor home so Alphonse stayed with him and Orly brought her over to Chaplain John's place.

John was funny. He had opened the door, seen Orly, and said, "Next."

Orly had laughed. "You been busy tonight, John, or what?"

John replied, "Mostly 'or what,' Orly. What you got here?"

He had come to the door in his bathrobe, looking very sleepy. Martha was right behind him and quickly took over making Alicia very comfortable in the extra bunk.

As she orientated herself Alicia groaned out loud. "Oh, I have to call my mom." She looked at her watch and swung her feet over the edge of the bunk. "I am in so much trouble."

Martha was at the stove when she heard Alicia stirring. She leaned back from the stove and said, "Well, good morning. I hope you slept well. I bet you need to call home. The phone is right there on the table, so help yourself."

"Thank you," Alicia mumbled as she took the phone and dialed home.

155

"Hi, Mom, it's me. No, I am okay, Mom . . . I'm sorry, Mom . . . Mom, please don't talk Chinese. I can't keep up with you." *Oh, man,* thought Alicia. *I am in big trouble.* Mom only spoke Chinese when she was really steamed and couldn't think fast enough to speak English.

When Alicia explained that she had spent the night in a chaplain's motor home with him and his wife, her mom calmed down somewhat. Then Martha had taken the phone and talked to her for a minute, telling her that Alicia was just fine. Finally Alicia managed to get off the phone with a promise to fill her mom in on all the details when she got home tonight. She also agreed to call Alphonse's mom and tell her he was okay. She breathed a big sigh of relief when she hung up the phone.

Alphonse woke up and looked at his surroundings. *This thing is plush,* he thought. *What a way to live. Wow! What a way to travel.*

Then he jumped out of bed in a panic. He looked out the window. It was broad daylight and the sun was shining brightly. "My car, I've got to get to my car. What if they tow it or something?" He quickly pulled his pants on and tied his shoes.

Orly was sitting at the table, drinking a cup of coffee. "What's the hurry?" he asked.

"I'm sorry, Mr. Mann, but I just remembered my car. Alicia and me, we stashed it in the trees last night. I hope nobody found it and towed it away or something. It's not much of a car really, but it's all I got."

Orly nodded his head and rummaged around in some papers on the table. "Here, this is a parking permit and a pass for the compound. You can get your car and park it in here. After that, go over to John's motor home and get Alicia. Then you can go over to that motor home right there," Orly pointed out the window. "The one that looks like a big office. Go in there and see Helen Knight in Public Relations and tell her Orly Mann said to give you guys the 37A Treatment. Can you remember that, the 37A Treatment?"

"Yes, Mr. Mann, the 37A treatment. Thank you, Mr. Mann. Thanks for letting me sleep here. Thanks for everything, Mr. Mann."

"The name is Orly, Alphonse. You were a good friend to Alicia, and good friends don't come easy. Now get going before they find your car and tow it somewhere."

Instead of climbing the fence, Alphonse went out the gate this time. Security gave him a cursory look but he waved the pass back and forth. He found his little car with no problem and was relieved to see that no one had bothered it. The antenna was indeed broken and there were a few new scratches on the roof from the chain, but it just gave the little machine more character. He managed to find the right road and worked himself back to the motorhome compound. He flashed the pass and the security people said nothing as they waved him through. He found a parking spot between a brand-new Cadillac with gold flecked paint and a robin's egg blue Lincoln Town Car. He carefully rolled the windows up and locked the doors, wiped a smudge off the glass with his sleeve, and walked over to get Alicia. He looked back over his shoulder at his car. *Looks good setting there in the midst of all that expensive Detroit iron,* he thought.

It seemed that everyone was happy except Paolo. Bear was visibly excited, and Doug and his dad were talking together in low tones. There was a race to run today and everyone would be there except him. He disconsolately pulled on his jeans, still dirty from the work under the car last night. He had nothing to look forward to but another day in the Chicken Shack. The crowd was expected to be enormous. Something over 130,000 people, Bear said. No doubt every one of them would want fried chicken, and he would have to clean it, cook it, and serve it. He shuddered.

Dad would probably forget to record the race for him. He had trouble with the VCR anyway, and Paolo wouldn't even get to see the race secondhand. Then he still had to get that stupid shift linkage fixed somehow. Doug would probably have a lot of other things to do once the race was over, and Paolo would be stuck here for a week.

Bear was yelling for everybody to get going. He and Bud headed out the door and walked quickly down the hill toward the garage area with their heads together, talking.

"Come on, Paolo, we'll go over to the hospitality tent and get some breakfast. What's the matter with you? You look like you swallowed a bug or something."

Doug's effervescence was irritating. Didn't he know that Paolo had to work? Doug had an exciting day in front of him. This time, however, Paolo kept his mouth shut and put a smile on his face. After getting dressed, the boys headed out of the motor home into the fresh new morning.

"Oh, man, Doug. I'm so happy for you that your dad is back. Where has he been anyway? Is he okay?" asked Paolo. He was indeed genuinely happy for his friend.

"It's a long story, Paolo, but yeah, he is back and he is just fine. I guess I understand why he left, but I still don't understand why he wouldn't tell me where he was going," Doug said. "We'll work it out though."

Then Doug pointed to a group of people eating breakfast off paper plates in the hospitality tent.

"Paolo, look! Isn't that Alicia and Alphonse sitting there with Chaplain John and Martha?"

Paolo couldn't believe his eyes. Alphonse was demolishing a large stack of hotcakes, but the thing that jumped out at him was the fact that they were both wearing Orly Mann team jackets. Not only that, but around their necks were guest garage passes marked VIP.

As Doug and Paolo walked up, Doug said, "Hey, guys, how'd you get here? I see you got the 37A VIP treatment. The only way you get that is through Orly. I'm impressed."

Paolo stood with his mouth open. Alicia smiled at him. "Hi, Pally. I bet you are surprised to see us, huh? What a night we've had"—she was interrupted by Alphonse, who spoke around a mouthful of food.

"Paolo, this racing stuff is pretty good. I slept in Orly Mann's motor home last night and I gotta tell you, it's pretty nice. Look, my car is parked right over there with all those big expensive cars. And we got these passes so we can watch the race from just about anywhere, and we

159

get free food and everything." He paused and took another big mouthful of pancakes.

Paolo remained speechless as he listened to their story. He didn't say a word when Alicia told him of the mistake she had made copying the letter. He could tell that she was truly embarrassed. He listened to the rest of her story, with constant interruptions from Alphonse, and pieced it together in his mind. *At least she did her best to make the situation better. She really went out on a limb coming out here in the middle of the night,* Paolo thought.

There was an excitement in the air as the crowd poured into the racetrack. The intensity was starting to build. The garage area was frantic with activity as mechanics swarmed all over the race cars like workers around a queen bee. This was the money day—the day when the big prizes would be awarded and optimism grew in the hearts of all the competitors. At this stage of the race every team in the field still had a chance to win and every crew was paying meticulous attention to the details that might change the outcome. Right now the playing field was level. As soon as the race started reality would set in, and it would quickly become evident who was fast and who wasn't.

Crews began to transfer equipment to the working pits. Each crew was given a carefully marked-out area in which to keep their tools, tires, gas cans, and all the assorted equipment needed to cover any eventuality during the course of the three-hour race. The pole-sitter, because he had qualified with the fastest time, was in the first stall. Behind him came the next fastest qualifier and so forth until the slowest qualifier was clear at the other end of the pit lane.

Orly was a ways back in twenty-fourth, but it didn't matter. Things would equal out as the cars made their stops. Everybody ultimately drove the same distance down the pit lane. It didn't really matter where they stopped. What really mattered was how quick the crew got him out.

Some of the crews were pushing their "war wagon" into place and setting up the electronic and pneumatic equipment. The war wagons were immense toolboxes on large rubber wheels, and every crew had one painted in their team colors. Orly's was orange and yellow and shone with a fresh coat of wax that highlighted the purple trim. Bear made sure the crew paid attention to every detail.

Some had brackets on the top that held captain's chairs so the crew chiefs could sit above the pits and keep track of the action. Many crews had personnel that sat beside the crew chief with a laptop computer system to record scoring, fuel, mileage, and the general chaos that punctuated a race. The war wagons also held a satellite dish and a TV monitor so the crews could watch the race through the television network feed.

Down low they also held the air tanks that powered the high-speed impact wrenches that the tire men used. These were pneumatic guns used to loosen and tighten the lug nuts that held the wheels on the car. They kicked like a ten-gauge shotgun and had to be held with two hands because of the two hundred pounds of air pressure that tortured their screaming bearings and spun them at fantastic rpms.

The jackman had already carefully oiled his lightweight jack that was designed to raise the car off the ground in two gut-wrenching pumps on the four-foot handle. He had to be the quickest on his feet because in a four-tire stop, he had to switch from one side of the car to the other. He was like a middle linebacker on a football team—in the center of the action, keeping an eye on how everybody was doing their job. When he dropped the jack it was the signal for the driver to hit the throttle and go screeching back into the race.

The tire man, whose sole job was to keep track of the rubber, had four sets of tires laid out in the back of the stall and he was carefully checking air pressure. In a few minutes he would glue five lug nuts on each wheel so that when the wheel was thrown on the hub, the tire changer could simply squeeze the air wrench in five short bursts and lock it onto the car. Each tire was carefully marked so that everyone knew exactly when and where it should go on the car.

On the racing side of the pit wall, the pit stalls were marked out with thick-painted white lines and treated like holy ground. Every inch was carefully swept so no offending piece of dirt or gravel could impede anyone's movement. It was kept immaculate and powder dry through the course of the race. Even the tiniest drop of moisture was quickly sponged up. When a tire was fresh off the racetrack it was gummy with heat, and any type of moisture made it slick as glass. Slick tires meant no traction, and no one wanted a 3,400-pound out-of-control missile sliding through the pit stall. Men had been killed in just such a fashion. Any time a man was on the *angry* side of the pit wall, he had to be doubly cautious and keep his wits about him. Bear carried a nasty scar on his calf from being catapulted over the pit wall by an out-of-control race car.

During the course of a race, the cars would come down the pit lane to a certain point and then have to slow to a speed designated by NASCAR. It varied from track to track, depending on the width of the lane and so forth, and cut down on the danger to the crews.

The crew men would stand poised on the pit wall with air wrenches and gas cans at the ready. Then they would fly over the wall, in a carefully orchestrated ballet, to change tires and add fuel and refreshment to the panting cars in movement so quick and coordinated it was hard to follow. In seventeen to nineteen seconds, if all went well, the cars would again roar up the pit lane, re-tired and refueled, at their designated speed, to reenter the fray.

Paolo finished his breakfast and slid his chair back. "Well, I'll be seeing you guys. I've got to get over to the Chicken Shack and get busy."

"Man, that's not fair, Paolo. What a drag that you have to work. Can't you get out of it somehow?" asked Alphonse.

"No, I can't. Uncle Rollie needs me. Look at this crowd coming in here. He's going to need all the help he can get. I'm stuck," Paolo said with a glum look on his face.

"Hey, Paolo, I've got your shift linkage. I'll get Shorty or one of the guys to weld it real quick. Won't take a minute. Me and my dad are going to stay around here tonight and then drive back cross-country tomorrow, so I can help you put it back on after the race," said Doug in a rush.

"Thanks, Doug, I would appreciate that. Well, gotta go."

Alicia pushed her chair back and said, "Come on, Pally, I'll walk down there with you."

They headed out of the compound walking side by side.

"Paolo, I'm sorry about the whole thing with that paper. I was trying to show off. I didn't mean to be a smart aleck. I hope you aren't mad at me," Alicia said as she tugged on his arm to make him stop so she could look up into his face. "Do you forgive me, Paolo?"

He looked down into her sincere face. "Alicia, I forgive you. I have done some real stupid stuff myself in the last couple of days. I'm not so good myself."

"Thanks, Pally. I couldn't stand it if you were mad at me." She tugged his arm even tighter and pulled his face down to her and kissed his cheek. The coolness of her lips made his ears burn.

They continued to walk toward the Chicken Shack. When they arrived, Paolo took a deep breath as if he was going to jump off a very high diving board and said, "Well, I'll see you later, Alicia."

"Bye, Pally," she said. She waited until he went in the back door and then looked around for a clean place to sit down and wait.

Uncle Rollie greeted him as he came in the back door. "Hey, Pally, nice to see you. Did you get the car fixed? Sleep okay? How you doing? Pally, I got some news for you." Uncle Rollie went on without a breath, "Pally, I got a problem—I've got to fire you. So I would appreciate it if you would get out of here." He winked at Paolo. "See,

164

Paolo, I got these other people to help me today." He motioned over his shoulder where Paolo could indeed see that there were four new faces in the back.

"So, I hope you understand I really don't have a place for you now. I hope it's okay." Rollie went on, "Oh, by the way, some nice lady came by a few minutes ago and dropped off a package for you. Here it is." Uncle Rollie handed him a large bag that was sealed at the top and had 37A, Paolo Pelligrini written on the front. "You can change back there. Now get out of here." He finished by giving Paolo a slap on the back.

Paolo took the bag and opened it quickly. Inside was an Orly Mann team uniform, with the name Paolo embroidered over the pocket, an official Orly Mann team jacket, and at the very bottom of the bag a garage pass marked VIP.

Five minutes later it was a different Paolo that came flying out the back door of the Chicken Shack. Alicia stood up as Paolo turned in a circle.

"How do I look?" he asked. Then he said in an accusing tone, "You had something to do with this, right?"

"Well, sort of, I suppose. I did mention to Orly that you were a real fan and a good friend of Doug's. He's the one who did it really."

"Thanks, Alicia, I can't tell you what this means to me. I have been dreaming of this day for I don't know how long."

"I know, Pally. You look pretty good," said Alicia as she took his hand in hers.

Together they left the back of the Chicken Shack and walked toward the garage area hand in hand. With big smiles, they flashed their passes at the security people as they headed toward Orly's hauler.

🏁🏁

Orly stepped out of the shower and toweled off. Then he began meticulously, almost ritually, getting dressed. The ribs were still sore and his bad leg throbbed a little today. It was familiar pain and he was used to it. He pulled his stuff out of the closest and laid it out on the bed.

First came the flameproof long underwear. He pulled them on carefully and smoothed out the wrinkles around his back and hips. It could get hot, but if there was a crash and a fire it would give him a few more seconds of protection. Not a lot but some. Then he pulled on the flameproof socks and wiggled his toes. They made his feet sweat a little but the extra protection was worth it. Burned feet were incredibly painful. He knew that for a fact. As he pulled the socks up he examined the burn scars that covered his lower legs. A few years ago Orly had been working in the shop when he inadvertently spilled some gasoline on his pants. He didn't even know he had done it until all of a sudden they caught fire. It burned his ankles and calves pretty good and also made him determined to never get burned again. Then he finally slipped on the one-piece hand-tailored driving suit. It was custom fit and looked like a walking billboard with the many sponsor logos all over it. He left the collar undone. There would be plenty of time to close it tightly under his helmet. Orly thought that getting dressed for a modern-day race was a lot like medieval knights putting on armor for battle. *I bet all that metal was hot, just like a driving suit,* Orly thought.

166

Even though he hadn't had a lot of sleep, he still felt good. They had finally gotten the suspension thing figured out for sure. Now maybe they could concentrate on racing. He felt rested and calm. Well, not entirely. There was a ball of excitement in the pit of his stomach. He smiled and greeted it like an old friend. It was a familiar feeling, one that gave him an indication that this might be a pretty good day. Who knew? It was in God's hands.

He put on a pair of sneakers and picked up his bag, which contained his helmet and driving shoes. *Time to go do battle,* he thought, as he stepped out the door of the motor home. He joined a few of the other drivers leaving the compound on their way to the drivers' meeting in the garage area.

Whatever you do, work at it with all your heart, as working for the Lord, not for men.

Colossians 3:23

"Everybody else has had good days and we've had a couple of bad days to put us back, so if we just have good days from now on we'll be all right."

Jeremy Mayfield, Winston Cup driver, car #12

THE FANS HAD come here by the tens of thousands and the place was crawling with excitement like an overturned ant hill in a flash flood. Every grandstand was filled to capacity and there were thousands of folks standing four deep at the fences all around the asphalt ribbon, which was the field of battle. The brown hills were covered with people sitting on blankets and lawn chairs. From a distance they looked like layers of confetti on a brown backdrop.

The multi-colored race cars marked for war with numbers and decals sat mute in formation on the pit lane waiting patiently for their drivers. Their windshields were covered to keep the early afternoon sun from heating their interiors. It was a symbolic gesture because in a few minutes the hot exhaust from the dynamite-laden racing engines would turn them into pressure cookers anyway.

The national anthem had been sung, the sky divers floated to the earth, landing on the front straightaway in perfect formation. Even the three F–16s from the nearby Air Force base had made their low-level pass over the crowd, causing everyone to inadvertently duck. The hot cherry red of their jet exhaust was a portent of things to come. The preliminaries were over and nothing was left . . . except the race.

Doug, Alphonse, Alicia, and Paolo all stood on the top of the hauler with a good view of most of the track. Everybody had earphones and could listen to the radio transmissions, but no one had a transmitter except Doug. He was all business and paid attention to no one as he sorted his watches and lap sheets. Alicia and Alphonse were nervous and made stupid jokes until finally Paolo looked at them with his finger to his lips. They didn't know what to expect, but he did. He gently patted Doug on the back and gave him a thumbs-up. Doug was visibly tense.

Bear was happy. He had torn the front suspension apart first thing this morning and put it right. Right bearings, right grease, fresh brake pads, a toe-in adjustment, and then he gave it all a very serious talking to. In the process he relied on his experience as crew chief, making a couple other minor changes that he knew would bear fruit later in the day.

He smiled when he saw Bud come sauntering down the hill. The rest of the crew was delighted to see him, and there was a lot of back slapping and high-fiving going on when Bud entered the pits.

Bear surveyed the pit stall area. This was the working pits. The tires were carefully laid out and everything that could be checked had been double- and triple-checked. Everything was in place, and they were as ready as they could be. Bear hummed to himself. *Boy, racin' sure is fun,* he thought.

Orly made small talk with the other drivers while they all waited to be introduced to the crowd. He felt loose but tense, which was his best combination. When his turn came to walk across the platform that was full of local dignitaries, he did it quickly and with little fanfare. He waved briefly during a round of applause from that part of the crowd paying attention, then walked off with long-legged strides to the pit lane.

Normally Orly accommodated anyone who wanted an autograph but not today. He waved a couple of people off in a gentle manner and headed for the car. He could see it sitting there, its orange and yellow paint scheme with the large 37 painted on the side and the roof. The Speed King sponsor logo covered the hood. Other sponsor logos and decals for oil companies, spark plugs, tires, all kinds of things, were on the front fenders. Decals were important. They paid contingency money. If there was no decal then there was no payoff. Every little bit in the pot helped pay the expenses.

Just over the driver's door, on the edge of the roof, was his name written in purple script: *ORLY.* It still gave him a little flash of thrill when he saw it painted on the car. As he got closer he saw that the crew had added some flourishes and a few little twinkley stars in chrome silver paint. NASCAR wouldn't like that. They had strict regulations about that kind of stuff. But it was a way for the crew to let Orly know that they were glad to have the suspension thing fixed and that they were supporting him. He was eager to get into the car and quiet his nerves.

Finally after the agony of waiting, it was time for the drivers to climb into their cars. Orly liked this time of peace before the storm. His ribs were better today as he slid through the window in a fluid motion. He settled in his seat and adjusted his belts, making sure the tube to his water bottle was within reach and plugging in his radio. He adjusted his goggles and polished them quickly with the cloth he kept tucked in his driver's suit, then raised the window net up and snapped it into place. Finally he just sat with his hands folded loosely in his lap. Collecting his thoughts, he enjoyed the isolation. The crew pulled off the windshield cover and he squinted momentarily in the bright sunlight. He waved the media crew right on by. He wasn't in the mood for an interview just right now. Maybe after the race. That was if they wanted to talk to him. It all depended on how he finished.

The command came suddenly from some bigwig or other propped up just for this occasion, "Gentlemen, start your engines." Orly hadn't heard a word of the other festivities, but he heard these words loud and clear. He flipped the switches, pushed the starter button, and the finely tuned engine caught on the first turn and came rumbling to life.

Bear's voice sounded in his ear. "What's it look like, Orly?" Bear meant the gauges on the dash.

"Everything is where it ought to be, Bear," Orly replied.

"How's the ribs?"

"I'm okay, Bear. Quit fussin'."

"Okay, okay, Orly. Just remember we got one hundred twelve laps to get to the front, so be patient and stay out of trouble. You know how it is, Orly. Some of these yahoos will be beating each other up in the first couple of laps to get to the front."

Orly didn't respond; he simply clicked the mike button once.

Bear was obviously nervous and needed to talk. "You up there, Jimmy?"

"Yup, I'm here, Bear," said Jimmy curtly, as if he could sense Orly's quiet, determined focus.

Bear finally quit talking on the radio and there was quiet. The tension mounted as Orly waited to go.

Then the pace car pulled out with all its lights flashing and two by two the race cars rumbled past, shaking the ground. Orly settled himself in the seat and looked around the inside of the car, taking stock of everything as they completed the first parade lap. He noticed the crowd for the first time and waved his hand out the window as did all the other drivers. He glanced around the inside of the car again. Everything looked and smelled good. A race car driver depended a lot on his nose. Burning oil or an overheated engine had a peculiar smell, and a good driver used every tool available to be aware of his surroundings.

He was sitting in a highly crafted custom machine. It could take him to victory or with no warning, it could hurt him big time. Even worse, it could snuff the life out of him if he wasn't aware every second of what he was doing.

"Two or three, Bear?" Orly asked in the radio, meaning how many parade laps would there be before the race started.

"Three, Orly," said Bear.

"Can you see me good, Jimmy?" asked Orly.

"Yup, I gotcha. The 4 car two rows ahead of you is smoking some when he lets off. Might be leaking something. I'll let you know."

Orly clicked the mike button twice.

On the first lap the pace was agonizingly slow. The speed picked up some on the second lap, and just about flat out on the third. Halfway through the third lap the pace car's flashing strobe lights went out which meant, "Get ready, boys!" The brightly colored race cars loafed along behind, patiently biding their time. Some of the drivers were moving their cars back and forth in arcs, trying to work some heat into their tires. As the pace car came through turn ten for the third parade lap, it dove down the pit lane seeking a safe haven. The pole-sitter held the pace and then accelerated slowly toward the flag station at the start-finish line with the field bunched tightly behind him. The starter had the green flag hidden behind his right leg as the pack came loping toward him. He pointed his empty left hand at the pack like a traffic cop for a long agonizing second . . . then whipped the green flag out in his right hand and waved it vigorously. The race was on!

A sudden wave of awesome thunder rolled over the valley as every driver in the field stood as hard as they could on the gas pedal at the same time. Bear's voice crackled in Orly's earphones, "Green flag, Orly."

The race started just about the way Orly thought it would. He knew that he would have to be patient. As he ran up into turn two he felt a bump as the driver behind him misjudged the corner. Guys were already pushing and shoving trying to move up in the field. Orly had no place to go until the pack sorted itself out a little. He was careful to stay out of trouble. A car behind him tried to outbrake him on cold tires going over the hill into the chute and promptly fishtailed off into the dirt. Orly coolly avoided him by a matter of inches and thought nothing of the close call.

Things stayed together for the first ten laps as the field began to string out and Orly began to get into his rhythm with some space to work. Then, just ahead of him, Jimmy's prophecy was fulfilled as the engine on the 4 car started smoking and scattering busted parts across the track. It tore hoses and fittings and hemorrhaged every bit of oil and coolant on board. This lifeblood, along with an assortment of expensive twisted parts, slicked down the corner pretty good.

Jimmy's words came too late, "Oil all over . . ."

Orly was in the mess before Jimmy had a chance to finish. He managed to avoid most of the debris and unconsciously corrected the wild gyrations of the car as the tires lost adhesion. In the process he sensed as well as heard a tinny ting as something bounced off the bottom of his car.

He felt the change in the tire's performance immediately and keyed the mike. "Cut a tire. Left side I think."

The crew jumped into frenzied activity as they copied the message on their headsets. "Okay, boys, you heard him. Let's make sure it's the left side. Everybody keep their eyes open real good," said Bear.

"Bear, I can see what he ran over and I think he hit it with the left rear. The car looks okay, though," said Jimmy from his perch on the hill.

"Are they gonna throw a full-course yellow?" asked Orly. A full-course yellow meant that the whole racetrack would be under the yellow flag and every car would have to hold their position after they crossed the start-finish line. If it wasn't a full-course yellow then it would only be a local-yellow flag situation that would affect only that corner—the cars would not be allowed to pass in that corner only. Once the corner crews had things under control the yellow flags would be put away and things would go back to normal.

Jimmy was watching the starter on his perch over the track through his binoculars, and so was Doug. The starter was the key. As Jimmy watched, the flagman held the headset to his ear with one hand and reached for the yellow flag. As the leaders came around, he waved the yellow flag vigorously.

"Full course, Orly. Get in and get out," said Bear. If Orly came in under yellow he would lose a few positions but he wouldn't lose a lap. He could rejoin the field at the tail end. The crew couldn't dilly around though.

In the meantime, Orly had his hands full fighting the flat tire. Racing tires had an inner liner that kept them from

175

going completely flat but the car was still pretty squirrelly. He hugged the outside of the track as he came down the esses, through turn ten, and into the pit lane.

"Watch your speed, Orly," said Bear in his ear. Coming down the pit lane too fast had a price. It could cost a thirty-second penalty, which in turn could cost a lap. There was a black line on Orly's tachometer that told him where to hold the revs in second gear as he rumbled down the strip.

"Watch your mark, Orly. Got the sign?" asked Bear. "Left sides only, boys. We have to get him out quick now."

One of the crewmen was holding a long pole out in front of the pit stall with a cutout in the shape of the number 37. He was waving it gently so Orly would know exactly where his pit stall was. Orly slid the car to a stop dead on the money and the waiting crew was over the wall like Marines attacking a beachhead.

An assigned NASCAR official stood off to the side watching every move. It was his job to make sure there were only six guys over the wall and all the lug nuts were on and tightened before the car left the pits. Mistakes in the heat of battle were common. Leaving a lug nut loose would incur a penalty. Leaving two or three loose could cause a wheel to come off—and provide footage for an embarrassing moment on somebody's bloopers film. If too many guys came over the wall they would be penalized a lap. Running over an air hose would cost a lap too.

The crew was as graceful as ballet dancers as the jack man slid the jack under the car at the yellow tape marking the midpoint and gave it two hard pumps. The tire changers, their air hoses snaking behind them like umbilical cords to the war wagon, slid to their kneepads in front of the wheels with their air guns firing. By the time the car was in the air, both the front and rear tires were off and the tire handlers had positioned new ones to go back on. The old ones were given a backward push and a crewman leaned over the wall and snatched them up and out of the way. The air wrenches screamed, and then both Bud and the rear tire changer threw their hands in the air signaling that they were done. Bud took a quick look under the car to see if anything had been damaged. He gave a quick thumbs-up to Bear.

In the meantime the gas man had plugged his red, eleven-gallon fuel can into the gas tank fitting and the catch man, who was standing just off to his right at the back of the car, plugged his catch can into the overflow valve. First, air came hissing out of the check valve on the fuel tank as it was displaced by the rushing fuel. Then the air turned to a mist and finally raw gasoline came spilling out signaling that the tank was as full as possible. The catch man threw his hand up and both he and the gas man stepped back. The car didn't take much fuel because they had only run a few laps, but every drop would be accounted for. The cans would be weighed on a special scale to record exactly how much fuel went into the car and how much was remaining. It could make the difference later on.

During the pit stop, Bear sat on top of the war wagon, watching everything and everybody at the same time. As soon as the jack man heard Bear's definitive "now," he dropped the car and pulled the jack out of the way. This was the signal for Orly to spin the tires as he headed down the pit lane toward the track, picking up speed as he worked through the gears. He held his speed until he crossed the white line and the official waved the green Go paddle at him, then dynamited the gas.

"Not bad boys. Good job," said Bear.

One crewman was quickly over the wall with a broom and every inch of the stall was carefully swept. He picked up the discarded lug nuts and carefully counted them.

Orly caught up with the tail end of the field on the back side of the course and idled along behind. Now instead of twenty-fourth he was forty-first or fifty-seventh or something. Whatever he was, it was a long way back from the leaders. But he wasn't dead last. Several cars had used the opportunity to pit and make adjustments too.

"Good job on the stop, guys. Did you find the hole, Bear?" asked Orly.

"Yeah, we got it, Orly. Was the rear." It was very difficult to determine which tire was flat. Sometimes, but not always, it was easy to tell which side the flat was on but very difficult to know exactly whether it was front or rear.

"We'll make it up. We've got lots of time," said Bear.

"Yeah, and no place to go but forward," said Orly. "What place we in, Doug?"

Doug was ready. He had been extremely busy watching cars pit and watching the scoring tower at the same time. "Thirty-sixth, Orly. Right now everybody is on the same lap. The 4 car is out."

"Get ready, Orly. The green is coming out next lap," said Jimmy.

This time the start would be single file, and Orly was ready. Bear again carefully watched the flagman. "Green, go," he said in a calm voice. Orly nailed the start and went by two cars through the sweeping turn one on the way up to turn two. The race stayed green for the next thirty laps and Orly picked up his rhythm. The car was good, excellent in fact. He passed carefully but decidedly. It wasn't easy to get around other cars on the twisty course, but Orly took advantage of every opportunity. He would dog the car ahead of him, hanging just off his rear bumper, then a little slip, a little bobble going in or coming out of the corner, and Orly shoved his way past.

Jimmy was always a little ahead of him, giving him pertinent information.

"Clear, Orly. You got him," Jimmy said as Orly passed a car coming out of turn eleven. "The 6 car is next. He seems to be running out of brakes. Try the inside," said Jimmy. "You'll be coming up on a lapped car next. He has been in and out of the pits several times. I'll let you know."

Occasionally he would have to fall in behind another car for a lap or two, waiting for just the right opportunity. When it didn't come soon enough to suit him, he wasn't adverse to a little nudge going into a corner. Just a little I'm-here-get-out-of-the-way tap.

In the meantime, the front of the race had turned into a train with five cars running nose to tail. They were being patient for now but they were race car drivers and each guy knew for certain that he could lead this thing, given the opportunity. But race car drivers never gave away anything and whatever they got they would have to earn . . . or take. The fourth place guy was moving slightly back and forth as if just trying to hold his position. The sweat was running off him in rivers as he banged the gearshift and sawed the steering wheel. His spotter was yelling in his ear about this and that. Way down deep in his heart he wished the guy would shut up but he was too busy to push the mike button.

Alicia was learning. She was amazed that Paolo didn't mind answering her questions. Both she and Alphonse were beginning to figure out what was going on. The constant radio chatter helped some, but she sure didn't realize that so much could go on all at once. Occasionally she could hear the PA system and this helped some too.

"Paolo, Orly got fuel when they stopped, right?" she asked.

"Right, Alicia. He topped off the tank but he only took left side tires which means that the right side ones are getting pretty worn by now," Paolo said.

"Why didn't they put on right side tires?" she questioned.

"Bear didn't want to take the time. A two-tire stop is a lot faster than a four. He knew they could pass a couple of cars in the pits and besides, they only had a few laps on them," Paolo replied.

"When will they stop again?" Alica asked.

"Pretty soon," Paolo replied. "Everybody will be stopping in about ten laps. I don't know if Bear will keep Orly out longer or bring him in when the leaders stop. Some guys are talking about making it a two-stop race. You know, only two pit stops, but I heard Bear say that he didn't think anybody could do it on two stops. If they made it a two-stop race, they would have to stop after lap fifty-six, which would be halfway." Then he added, "Fuel isn't the big problem. The problem is tires, and you can tell from watching

180

some of the cars that they are starting to go away—I mean, the tires are wearing out."

Several cars were noticeably fishtailing through the corners as the Goodyear Eagles wore out and the track got greasy from the accumulated rubber and oil.

"What lap are we on now?" Alphonse asked.

Paolo looked over Doug's shoulder and Doug tapped his scoring sheet with his pencil, pointing out the lap number.

"Lap forty-two, Alphonse."

"What place is Orly in now?" Alicia said.

Doug held up his fingers in a two and a one.

"Twenty-first and he has been moving up steady," said Paolo.

About that time the first three cars peeled off the track and came down the pit lane nose to tail. The fourth place car took over the lead, picking up five bonus points for leading. The fifth place car moved to the inside on turn eleven in an attempt to snatch the lead. The driver miscalculated, though, and the cars touched through the apex of the corner and both spun in a cloud of smoke. The corner marshals waved their yellow flags as the rest of the pack came thundering through.

Orly had plenty of warning as Jimmy alerted him on the radio.

"Keep it tight, Orly. They are just sittin' there in the corner, trying to get refired. I don't see no loose parts," he said. He meant debris on the racetrack. They certainly didn't need another blown tire. The tires were getting thin anyway.

"How's the tires, Orly?" asked Bear.

"Starting to go away big time, Bear."

"Okay, Orly, bring it in in three laps. What else you need?" Bear asked.

"Don't touch nothing but maybe bump the air pressure in the left front. Just a little, though. This thing is really hauling. I think it's better than the primary car was. Oh yeah, pull the sheet off the windshield. It's getting oiled up pretty good," said Orly. "How are the lap times, Doug?"

Everyone on the roof of the hauler looked expectantly at Doug. This was big stuff. Doug was talking to Orly Mann in the middle of a race and had just been asked a very important question.

Doug gave Orly some numbers. Then he added, "Orly, you are running as fast if not faster than the leaders when you get a clean track."

The radio clicked twice as Orly acknowledged and went back to work.

The cars that had spun out finally got refired and joined the back of the pack. *Two less we have to pass,* thought Bear. The three leading cars had pitted, and two had come out neck and neck to join the field. The third sat for agonizing seconds in the pits while the crew fought with a malfunctioning jack. Finally they got the car in the air but the mistake cost them valuable time, and when they were finished they were a lap down on the field. The driver burned rubber down the pit lane only to be black-flagged by the starter and given a stop-and-go penalty for violating the speed limit. This meant he would have to exit the racetrack and be held by an official at his pit stall for thirty seconds. It cost him another lap, so he was two laps down on the leaders. In this business, it didn't take long to go from third place to last.

"Next lap, Orly. Next time around. Got it?" said Bear. The mike clicked twice in his ear.

Orly was pitting on the forty-sixth lap and once again the Thunderbolt Ballet Company would perform their special choreography. This time it would be a green-flag, four-tire, full-fuel, certified NASCAR pit stop.

The crew was on the wall, waiting in eager, tense expectation as Orly came down the hill toward the pit exit. He entered the pit lane full speed, decelerating as he rounded the corner. He was dead on the money with the correct speed as he idled down to his stall. No faster than the limit, but by all means no slower either. The crew was over the wall in a flash of motion. Right side tires first. The jackman raised the car with two quick pumps, did a half turn to lay the old right rear tire on the ground, did a half turn back, and dropped the car. The gas man stayed out of the way as the right rear tire man ran by him to the left side. As soon as the air hose cleared he slammed the big gas can over the nozzle. As quick as the can went dry he did a half turn and tossed the empty can to a waiting crewman over the wall. No sooner had the empty can left his arms than it was replaced with another full one. Each can held eleven gallons, and the fuel tank held a maximum of twenty-two. He pirouetted with the second can in his arms and slammed it on the nozzle again. The jack dropped and he and the catch man ran a few steps with the car as it powered down the pit lane. Bud even had time before Orly accelerated to clean the grill of any debris that might impede the cooling air flow to the engine and front brake ducts. One of the tire handlers pulled the tab on the clear plastic sheet covering the Lexan bulletproof windshield, peeling it off in half a second. When it came off it brought the accumulated oil and bugs with it and left Orly seeing a bright new world.

Orly took the opportunity to grab a swallow of water from his bottle. It was lukewarm but it was wet. He hated ice water in the middle of a race; it made his stomach hurt. When the plastic bottle was empty he poked it out the window around the window netting and put the full one that had been shoved to him through the window in the holder. Then he dumped the car in gear as the jack dropped and accelerated down the pit lane.

The high fives were punctuated with whoops as the crew celebrated a picture-perfect job. The crews next to them gave them congratulatory waves for a great performance. It was their quickest stop of the day and it pulled Orly up into the top ten.

Ten laps later two cars tangled in the chute and one ended up a twisted wreck stuffed in the dirt bank. Once again the pace car came out to lead the field around the track while the mess was cleared away. Orly was sitting in tenth, but this yellow flag would bunch the field. Bear's voice tickled his ear.

"How're the brakes, Orly?" he asked.

Orly could say whatever he wanted. Both he and Bear knew many others were listening. Orly wasn't about to be honest. They could speak clear and honest under green-flag conditions when there wasn't time to think too much. But this was a yellow flag, which was a lot like a calm in the middle of the storm. The field was just loafing around the track waiting for the corner crews to finish their work. In truth, the brakes were still functioning great. Orly had taken special care to save them for the end of the race. Brakes were a limited resource and must be used accordingly. Abuse them too much and they went away in a hurry.

The answer to Bear's question was in the clicks of the radio—two clicks followed by a pause and then a click meant "good." Anything else meant lousy. Orly sent the "good" code.

"Want any wedge next stop? Want me to put a spring rubber in or anything?" Bear asked, refering to handling changes that the car might need.

Orly answered, "You could give me about four rounds of wedge and put three spring rubbers in for me, Bear." He followed this message with the same code as before which meant "don't touch nothin'."

Doug looked at Paolo's furrowed brow and quizzical look. "They're funning, Paolo. You know it takes more than thirty seconds to put a spring rubber in, and Bear would never put in three at the same time. Hear the code—Orly's running fine for right now."

"Why are they doing that, Paolo?" Alicia joined the conversation.

"They are teasing the other guys that are probably listening to our channel and just letting everybody know that they know what they are doing. I guess you might call it a 'man' thing or something," said Paolo. "When Doug switches to different channels you will hear some of the other drivers doing the same thing."

"Oh," said Alicia, as if uncertain.

Alphonse did though, and smiled to himself. He knew exactly what they were doing. He did it all the time on the basketball court.

Doug raised his earpiece and spoke to the other young people around him. "It's just a game Orly and Bear play on yellow laps. It kind of lightens the tension some. They are just funning," he said again.

The next time around, the starter held up the crossed flags which meant that the race was half over.

... for the worker deserves his wages.

Luke 10:7

"The pit crew did an excellent job, so we're really proud of the pit crew and Mark, he drove a clean race. Everybody's racing their guts out at the end. We're pretty proud of it as bad as we were."

Jimmy Fennig, crew chief for Mark Martin,
Winston Cup driver, car #6

EVENTUALLY THE CREAM comes to the top. On any given Sunday there were usually only a few teams that had a genuine shot at winning the race. In past years it had been maybe only two or three that had taken home all the money. Now the purses were so large and the sponsorships so lucrative it made the competition more fierce. Now eight to ten teams had a chance to win, and sometimes under the right circumstances the number could increase to fifteen.

The Save Mart/Kragen 350 at Sears Point was no different. In the second half of the race the "good" were beginning to pull away and "the less than good" or lousy were falling off the pace. Orly was in the top ten and holding his own for now. Bear was happy but not satisfied. Considering all the adversity they had endured the past few weeks, a top-ten finish would be plenty okay. The car was working well, which was a tremendous encouragement. At least nothing had fallen off the car or broken so far. To Bear's trained eye Orly was just cruising. That was if you called screaming down the front straightaway through turn one at a hundred fifty-one miles an hour, then slowing the 3,400-pound projectile down to thirty-five miles an hour for turn two *cruising!* Then he was accelerating again, slowing for three, setting up four, and grabbing a little air as the car crested the hill and powered down the chute hanging on for turn seven. Cruising indeed! Then, of course, there was the carnival ride through the esses as Orly laid first the left side and then the right side wheels over the sloped curbs that marked the edge of the track. This had a tendency to lift the car in the air and make it want to fly, but Orly would catch it with a quick flick of the steering wheel and bring it under control, never lifting his foot from the gas pedal. He had been doing it lap after lap and Bear knew that he wasn't even aware of his own movements, just the overwhelming fact that the car directly in front of him was holding him up. Yeah, he was cruising alright. But cruising really meant that he wasn't abusing the car and he still had a little in reserve.

"Doug," said Orly.

"You are twelve seconds behind the leader and he's pulling away from everybody right now," Doug said, knowing exactly what Orly wanted. "Second is two seconds behind him. Third through sixth are a second behind second place. Seventh through ninth are spread out and you are on the rear bumper of ninth. You have seven, no make that eight seconds on eleventh."

The mike clicked twice.

"Everybody has to stop, Orly. We are back in sequence with the leaders. The 14 car is in seventh and he might go the distance, but I doubt it," Bear said. "Howzit all working? I'd like to bring you in with about twenty to go and give you fresh rubber. That would be in about twelve laps. What d'ya think?"

The mike clicked twice.

🏁🏁

Orly was thinking. Pit stops were coming up. Probably, if things stayed green, the first six cars would pit at the same time. Then it would be a mad dash to see which crew was the quickest and the order would be shuffled. The seventh place guy might try to stretch it. He would inherit the lead when the other guys pitted. He could lay back a little and save fuel and tires. Might work, but then probably not. Bear didn't think so and Bear knew what he was talking about. The eighth and ninth guys were starting to fall off the pace, and if he wasn't careful he would fall back with them. His car felt like it still had a lot left. It was simple. He needed to get past the two cars ahead of him if he was going to have any shot at the front. He had the best pit crew in the business, and if they gave him a good, no make that a *great* stop, he would be in the mix. He feathered the brakes a little going into turn two and gave the ninth place car a gentle tap.

Doug watched Orly close the gap on ninth place and looked over at Paolo. He raised his eyebrows as Paolo looked at him. He had seen it too. They both grinned.

Alicia saw the byplay and said, "What?"

"Watch close, Alicia. This race is going to get very exciting," Paolo replied.

Orly bided his time carefully, weighing his options in the midst of the thundering exhaust and heat in the car. As he and the ninth place car came up on a lapped car that was running on the inside of the track, they were both forced to slow. They came through turn ten and braked hard for turn eleven. Orly ducked to the inside and boxed the ninth place car behind the slower one and made a clean pass.

Jimmy's voice filled his head, "Clear! You got him, Orly."

"The 2 car is eighth Orly, and he is about seven-tenths ahead," said Doug.

Orly had a little open racetrack ahead of him and he used this to his advantage in two ways. First, he tested his car to see just how much he had left in the way of tires and brakes. The motor was strong and all the gauges were right on track. Second, he used every ounce of his skill and ability to whittle down the distance between him and the next car. It took him three laps to close the distance. The guy's spotter must have been sleeping or something. Orly came up on him in turn eleven, out-braked him going into the corner, and simply powered past him coming out. The driver looked surprised when Orly went by.

Again Jimmy's voice spoke, "Clear! You are in eighth spot, Orly."

"Seventh is the 12 car and he is five-tenths in front of you. You have been almost a second faster than the leaders the last three laps," said Doug.

Orly's mike clicked twice.

"Three laps, Orly. Three laps this time by," said Bear.

The mike clicked twice.

The seventh place car offered no resistance. He seemed to be playing the waiting game; it was a gamble. If he had enough fuel he would win. If he didn't he would finish back in the pack somewhere. His crew chief must've decided it was worth a try. His spotter apparently told him Orly was coming big time, because he just pulled over and let Orly go. Two laps later it didn't matter anymore because the "gambling driver" was in the pits, trying to get the transmission unstuck from second gear.

One lap later the fifth place car came slowly rolling down the pit lane trailing a terminal plume of smoke.

Alphonse pounded the rail of the observation platform with a closed fist. "Yesss. He's in sixth."

The front runners were closing up. The leader's tires had started to go and his two-second margin was shrinking. As a matter of fact, second through fifth were not only closing in on him but each other as well. Orly was coming, but he was still a second behind.

"Two laps, Orly," said Bear. Then he leaned over to Bud and lifted the mouthpiece on his radio. "I think they are all coming in at the same time. What you think?"

Bud looked up and down the pit lane at the stalls of the top five cars. They were starting to stir with action and excitement.

"Bear, you are right. Let's show them how to do it," he said with a grin. Then he turned and waved up at Doug on the hauler in the garage area. Doug waved back with a smile on his face.

Orly decided to use everything in the next two laps to get as close to the leaders as he could. At the end of one lap he had them in sight. The only problem was that there was a lapped car between him and them. As he came up on the slower car, the driver missed a shift with a balky transmission. Orly nearly rear-ended him as he suddenly slowed. He ducked to the inside but got clipped by the other car as he passed. It wasn't much but it bent the quarter panel into the rear tire, causing it to rub slightly. Jimmy saw it immediately.

"The left rear is rubbing, Bear. Left rear. It ain't rubbing much, Orly. Take it in. You got me, Bear?" said Jimmy.

"Yeah, I got you. Bring it in, Orly. Everybody is coming. Okay everybody, let's go to work. We've got to *bear down* now. We got to bear down hard." The crew looked at each other and smiled. They had been waiting to hear those words in their radio headsets. Old Bear Down was excited. That was good.

Bear came down off the war wagon and pulled a shortened baseball bat out of the bin on the toolbox.

"Paolo, Orly is coming in right?" asked Alicia.

"Yup, and so is everybody else. There are only nineteen laps left in the race and this is it. Orly has a tire rubbing on the left rear. If they don't fix the sheet metal it could wear through the sidewall of the tire and make it blow out. Racing tires don't have much of a sidewall. They make the sidewalls thin so the heat will go out. This is the last stop.

Even if it goes yellow no one will come in unless they absolutely have to," said Paolo.

"That looks like a baseball bat that Bear has in his hand. What is he going to do?"

"Just watch. You'll see. Here they come!"

The crowd of 130,000 plus was on its collective feet. Those that couldn't see the pit lane had their eyes glued to the giant screens placed strategically around the track. This was what made NASCAR racing so much fun. It wasn't just a battle on the track—it was a team effort. Whoever got in and out of the pits the quickest would have the best chance of winning. The race could be won or lost right there.

Orly had managed to catch the pack and tucked in behind the fourth place car as all five exited the track into the pit lane. Nose to tail they came around the corner to the pit stalls. The signs were out and waving and the crews were on the wall with air guns and gas cans at the ready.

"Gimme a short stop, Orly," said Bear into his radio.

Orly heard him and stopped a foot short of the mark. Bear was immediately over the wall and jammed the baseball bat between the tire and the fender. Orly was watching Bud and when Bear was positioned, he gave him a nod. Orly eased the clutch and the car moved forward a foot, which rotated the bat between the tire and the fender, bending it out. Bear pulled the bat out as the rest of the crew flew over the wall and went to work.

"That got it, Orly. Don't worry about it," said Bear catching his breath on the other side of the wall.

The whole operation took less than a second but it was enough to keep Orly from improving his position. It was too much time to make up and despite the world-class pit stop by the Thunderbolt Ballet Company, Orly was still in fifth when he went back out on the track. He nearly had fourth but he couldn't quite pull off the pass as he exited the pit lane and the other driver pulled out just ahead of him. He was a close fifth. In fact all five of the front runners were nose to tail.

This is it, thought Bear. *Now it's up to Orly. If we hadn't had to pull that panel out we coulda beat those guys.* Then he shrugged his shoulders and put it out of his mind. "That's racin'," he said out loud and resumed his perch on the war wagon to see how this thing was going to shake out.

The laps counted down. Paolo and Doug were so focused that there could have been an earthquake and they wouldn't have even noticed.

With twelve laps to go, the driver of the third-place car ran out of patience and tried a pass where he shouldn't have. As the five cars exited turn eleven in front of the pits, he ducked to the inside. The driver of the second-place car let his car drift out as he accelerated down the front straightaway toward turn one. This put the third-place car out in the marbles where the traction was tenuous, turning him down into the second-place car. They made contact and the second-place car bobbled for a second but managed to hang on with only a black donut on the right side to show for the bump. The third-place car was not so fortunate and immediately jumped sideways and backed hard into the concrete wall beneath the start-finish flag station. The impact spun the car around and it sat dead in the straightaway looking very much like someone had kicked it in the pants with a very hard oversized boot.

Orly had seen the driver ahead of him throw his hand up as he "checked up" by braking hard to dodge the out-of-control car. Orly got through just fine and everyone slowed as the yellow flag came out. The pace car pulled in front of the leader to set the yellow-flag pace.

"How long?" Orly asked, meaning how long would it be before they went back to racing.

"Two or three laps for sure, Orly. Breathe a minute," said Bear as he took his own advice and took a few deep breaths.

Everybody on the roof of the hauler thawed from their frozen state and eased cramped muscles. The accident had happened right in front of them and they were amazed to see the driver climb out of the car unhurt.

"Why did he crash, Paolo?" Alicia asked.

Paolo laughed. "Well, he got impatient because he thought the car in front of him was blocking him, so he tried to pass where he shouldn't have. He just ran out of room and lost it and backed into the wall. He hit it a ton though, didn't he?"

Alicia nodded her head.

🏁

Orly sat back in the seat and put his left hand out the window around the netting. He used his cupped palm to direct a stream of air inside the car.

He wiggled his neck some and eased his body. *The brakes are starting to go,* he thought. *They are getting a little spongy, and the pedal is soft.*

It took the workers six laps to get the track cleaned up and by that time the leaders were getting antsy. This thing wasn't over and all four of the professional drivers were convinced that they could better their position.

"Puts you in fourth, Orly," said Doug.

The mike clicked twice. Orly knew.

There was no radio traffic during this yellow flag. Everybody knew what needed to be done and the only one who could do it was Orly.

Bear couldn't sit still. He had moved from the top of the war wagon to the pit wall and back again. He had run out of words and the only thing left to do was to watch. If it were possible he would get out on the track and push the car to help Orly.

With six laps to go the pace car pulled off and the pack came around for the green flag once again. This time there were several back markers who were lined up on the inside, but they had sense enough to hang out of the way and let the four leaders go. The front runners ran nose to tail with everybody doing everything they possibly could to get by one another. Finally, the third-place car made an incredible move to get by the second-place car coming down the chute. There was no way Orly could follow him so he hung back in fourth. The passed driver wasn't about to give up and they pummeled each other for the next two laps.

"They are rubbing on each other pretty good, Orly. Watch out," said Jimmy's voice in his ear.

Orly could see that for himself. He obviously wanted to get around both of them but was reluctant for the moment to get too close. He saw it coming as they piled off the chute into turn seven side by side.

"No way," Orly said to himself.

As both cars fought for position, they slammed into each other. They separated for an instant and then slammed into each other again and both went sliding off the track into the dirt in a cloud of dust and tortured tire smoke. Orly feathered the throttle, ducked to the inside, and got by them both before they could collect themselves and get headed down the track. The leader was just ahead.

Jimmy's voice was calm. "There he is, Orly."

With two laps to go Orly held nothing back. He was so focused he could see nothing but the task in front of him. The brakes were now starting to go away big time. Orly used all of his experience and every ounce of his skill as he compensated for the lack of stopping ability by throwing the car sideways to slow it. A half a lap later he was knocking on the back door of the leader's house. As they flashed down through turn eleven for the next to the last time they were nose to tail. Orly tried the outside. No go. He just didn't have quite enough power to pull it off, so he ducked back behind.

They flashed under the start-finish line and the starter waved the white flag signifying one lap to go. No one within a three-mile distance was sitting down. People were whooping and hollering and pounding each other on the back.

Orly tried the inside of turn two. No go. Couldn't get it done. Through three. No way here. They crested the hill into four and both cars went airborne. Down the chute for the last time and through turn seven. Orly tried everything. Nothing worked. They blasted down the esses so close together that they looked like one car. They snaked down the hill through turn ten. No room to pass here, but both drivers were flat out, motors screaming and tires clawing for adhesion.

Turn eleven was the last chance. Everybody strained to see. Would Orly go to the inside or the outside? What would the other guy do to block him? Could Orly make it happen?

Alicia and Alphonse were screaming with excitement. Paolo was bouncing up and down, pounding the rail. Doug was watching in close-mouthed tenseness.

Jimmy and the rest of the spotters were all crowded together in a big bunch, trying to see.

Bear was down off the war wagon and standing on top of the pit lane, pounding Bud on the back.

The two cars came screaming down from turn ten to eleven. Orly ducked to the inside, waiting, waiting, waiting to hit the brakes. He downshifted using all the compression that the tortured engine could give him and hit the brakes hard. He did it! He had the lead!

Then the brake pedal went to the floor and he had to throw the car sideways to keep from hitting the wall. He scraped off just enough speed to make the corner, but the action allowed the other car to regain the lead. Orly gathered it together getting the car straight and powered out of the corner. Both cars came down the straightaway, screaming toward the finish line side by side as they put the power down. Then, the other car inched ahead by what seemed millimeters to finally take the checkered flag and the win by less than a foot.

Orly and the winner both backed off the gas as they went up the hill toward turn two. Orly pulled up beside him and gave him a congratulatory wave. He waved back and shook his right hand in the universal gesture that said, "Whew! That was close!" He had driven a smart race and earned the win. There would be other days. Finishing second wasn't the end of the world. It was a long season and second place money here at Sears Point wasn't so bad. After all the struggles they had been going through second was pretty good, actually.

"Orly, I'm getting too old for this," said Jimmy in his ear.

Orly smiled as he took down the window netting to let as much fresh air as possible into the car. He lifted his goggles from his eyes and wiped the sweat off his face. He tugged his gloves off, opened up the collar of his driving suit, and loosened his helmet strap. He listened for a minute and then realized he could hear the yells and applause of the crowd as he slowly circled the track on the cool-off lap.

"Jimmy might be too old for all this, but I like it! You done good, Orly. Next time we will start a little closer to the front so it won't be so difficult. Ain't racin' fun?" said Bear.

Orly clicked the mike twice. Then he said, "Thanks, Doug. Good job."

Doug clicked his transmitter twice.

The gang on top of the hauler was drained. As they took off their headsets and gathered their stuff the three rookies patted Doug on the back.

"Thanks, Doug," said Alicia. "I learned so much. I had the greatest time. Thanks for being our friend."

"Hey, man, I can't tell you how much I appreciate you giving us this experience. You are a great guy, Doug. I'm glad about your dad too. God really answered your prayers, didn't he?" said Alphonse.

"Yes, he did, Alphonse, and I am going to keep praying for yours. God taught me that I can trust him, and Jesus will teach me more, I think," Doug replied.

"Come on, Alicia, we've got to go. If we leave right this minute we can get a jump on some of the traffic," said Alphonse.

The group climbed down off the hauler. Alicia gave Doug a quick hug and then hugged Paolo as well.

"Call me when you get home, Pally. What time do you think it will be?"

"I don't know, Alicia. I still have to put my car together. It will probably be late. I'll call you. You guys get out of here and drive careful."

They turned and disappeared into the crowd. Doug watched them walk off, sad to see them go.

Epilogue

The faithless will be fully repaid for their ways, and the good man rewarded for his.

Proverbs 14:14

"I gave it all I had."

Davey Allison, 1961–1993, former Winston Cup driver

IT DOESN'T TAKE the circus long to leave town. The race hadn't been over for more than an hour before the used-up race cars were bedded down and stashed in the interiors of the haulers. They weren't clean and pristine anymore. As a matter of fact, many of them were not much more than junk.

The pit stalls were disassembled a lot faster than they had been put together. Everything was checked and then carefully stowed away in its proper place to be used another time. The crews were tired and the quicker the work was done, the quicker they could head home. It took only a short period of time to get the haulers ready for the open road. One by one they began leaving the garage area for the long nonstop trek back to North Carolina. They were in a hurry to get home and off-load. The Firecracker

400 was coming up at Daytona next week, and there was much to do between now and then.

Orly was still giving interviews after he and Bear had been pulled over to the winner's circle by the winner of the race. He was eager to share the glory with Orly. It had been a fantastic finish, and folks were still buzzing from the excitement.

Bear was enjoying himself. He and Orly and some of the other crew members would fly home tonight in Orly's airplane, so they could afford to hang around a little. It had been a pretty good weekend, all things considered. He was going to give Wiley a piece of his mind though. He nearly got Orly hurt. Should have given that letter to either him or Orly. Ah, well. Done now. The Prescotts got the money. He and Orly knew that was what the Lord would want them to do. That was good. Bud would get a share of today's winnings. That would help some too. Bear smiled as he signed yet another autograph. He wrote, "Bear," then put a little bear's face underneath it.

An hour later Orly sat in his motor home, drinking a soda. He was exhausted and his ribs throbbed with a dull ache. He had his shower and he was waiting for the aspirin to take effect. Dressed in street clothes, he was patiently waiting for Bear to come get him so they could go to the airport. Bud was sitting opposite him.

"So you and Doug will be in about Thursday, Bud?" Orly asked.

"Yes. Thanks, Orly, for letting us drive the motor home back together. It will give me a chance to explain some stuff to Doug about Peter and all." Then Bud went on, "Thanks too for letting me take off. I was pretty upset when I called you the night before I left. I knew you would understand."

"Family is the most important thing, Bud. Sometimes you just have to do what you have to. Even though some folks might not understand. Doug will understand," said Orly.

"Uh, Orly, I don't know how to say this, but thanks for the uh, gift, you know." Bud stammered and his face colored with embarrassment.

"Hey, Bud, I don't know what you are talking about.

"Here's Bear. Well, see you guys at the shop," Orly said as Bear came through the door. Bear was still smiling.

"Come on, race car driver, we got to go home and get ready for Daytona. See ya at home, Bud. Now, Orly, I was thinking if we took that track bar and moved the perch . . ." His voice trailed off as he and Orly went out the door.

Doug and Paolo sat on the ground with their backs against the side of Paolo's old Chevy. It was fixed but they were still sitting. The racetrack had emptied out and it was almost dark. The garage area was empty and even the cyclone fence around it was gone. Sears Point seemed lifeless in the twilight, and the only reminder of today's drama was the leftover tire rubber that marked the track's surface. In a few days it too would be gone. The place now looked like a badly organized dump with all the trash left by the thousands of people blowing around in the evening breeze.

203

Without moving Paolo said, "Well, I guess I better let you go, Doug."

"Yeah, I suppose. Dad will be down here looking for me in a while."

"What a race. Man, what a weekend. I can hardly wait to get home and see the replay on the VCR, that is if my dad got it for me." Paolo turned and looked at Doug.

"Doug, you are a great friend and I . . . well, I don't know what to say. I am so sorry that I got mad yesterday. I feel so bad." The intensity came through in Paolo's voice. "I learned a very tough lesson, though. And you are a special friend to still talk to me."

"Hey, Paolo, that's over with. I need to thank you for showing me how God works. You took time to pray with me and you showed what really matters to a Christian—people. You were my friend when I needed somebody to be a friend to me.

"You remember when Tom was teaching that lesson the other night. He talked about a friend '. . . sticking closer than a brother.' That's you, man. That's Jesus working through you, I think. Thanks for teaching me and showing me about Jesus." Doug stood up.

Paolo stood up too, and the boys looked at each other.

"I got your e-mail address, so I'll write you. Check it when you get home, okay?" said Paolo.

"Yeah, okay. I got yours too. Maybe I'll give you a blast from the motor home when we stop somewhere," said Doug.

"Do that and hey, Doug, go easy on your dad. He did what he had to do. Remember what the Lord Jesus would have you do . . . oops now I'm preaching," said Paolo with a chuckle.

Doug laughed too as he threw his leg over the scooter and gave it a kick. It started on the first try and both boys yelled in surprise.

"See you, Doug," said Paolo as Doug rode slowly off toward the now nearly empty motor home compound.

He stopped for a minute and turned and waved. "See you, friend," he shouted. "Thanks for being my brother."

> "And surely I am with you always, to the very end of the age."
>
> —Jesus (Matthew 28:20)